TALON EXTERMINATION

TALON
BOOK 5

BRENT TOWNS

ROUGH
EDGES
PRESS

Talon Extermination
Paperback Edition
Copyright © 2025 Brent Towns

Rough Edges Press
An Imprint of Wolfpack Publishing
1707 E. Diana Street
Tampa, FL 33610

roughedgespress.com

Paperback ISBN 978-1-68549-461-2
eBook ISBN 978-1-68549-460-5
LCCN 2025938548

TALON EXTERMINATION

TALON:

Anja Meyer
Jacob Hawk
Ilse Geller
Slania Albring
Marcus Gray

PREVIOUSLY...

HAWK WAS ABOUT to ask Lisa another question when Anja burst into the room. She slammed her cell on the table before grabbing Lisa Bennett by the hair and dragging her to her feet. Then, using her considerable strength, she slammed the British woman against the concrete wall and snarled, "Where is she, you fucking bitch?"

"Whoa, boss, what the hell is going on?" Hawk demanded.

"The phone, Jake."

"What about it?"

"Just look at the fucking phone," Anja roared, keeping her snarling face up close to Bennett's. "Where is she?"

Hawk picked up the cell and stared at the screen. There was a picture of a woman, mid-twenties, with blonde hair, and blue eyes. "Who is she?"

"She worked for German intelligence. Two years ago, she disappeared in Russia. No one knew where she went or what had happened to her. Until now."

"Yes, but who is she?" Hawk asked again.

Without taking her eyes off Lisa's, Anja said, "Marlene Roth."

"What is Marlene Roth to you?"

"She is my sister."

"Bollocks."

Somewhere in North Yemen

The unmaintained dirt road presented a rutted and rough ride for the passengers riding in the back of the truck, and they were jerked violently from side to side as the front wheels bounced from one hole to the next. Without a tarpaulin over the steel frame, the merciless sun beat down, further dehydrating the occupants. Marlene wiped at her dry, dust-caked lips, reopening a deep crack in them and making them bleed once more.

The truck lurched again, making the guard sway as he stood in the back, holding on to the overhead rail.

They had been driving through the desert for three days now, its heat overwhelming. Marlene's mind wandered due to the dehydration. Her eyes closed and then snapped back open as a jet thundered low overhead with a loud BOOM!

Their guard said something she couldn't understand and then laughed. He shifted his gaze and then said something to one of the women closer to him. She didn't answer. He shoved at her with a hand, and her head lolled to one side.

Dead? Fainted? Marlene couldn't tell. What she did know was that the woman was a British reporter who'd been accused of spying against the Russian regime and then locked away in one of their many political prisons. She had a husband and two children in Sheffield.

The guard poked at her again, then when he was unable to raise a response, slapped her face.

Still nothing.

With a grunt, he grabbed her by the shirt and began dragging her to the rear of the truck, eliciting shouts of protest and cries for mercy. He yelled something at them and then dropped the woman over the tailgate and onto the desert road.

Another jet passed low overhead, its booming roar almost deafening. Marlene leaned back and looked past the front of the truck in the bearing they were traveling.

At that time, the truck crested a ridge, revealing the snaking convoy of other vehicles all headed in the same direction. The same destination.

In the distance, a black and orange explosion was visible, the result of a bomb being dropped on the already devastated city. Before them, a large roiling mushroom rose into the air.

Then came the staccato sound of automatic gunfire.

Beside her, a woman asked in a low, crackling voice, "Do you know where we are going?"

Marlene turned her head and looked at the woman before responding, "We are going to hell."

———

Constanta, Romania

The group of five sat around a table, looking at each other. "We are all agreed?" Anja asked.

The others nodded. Hawk said, "Damn right."

"I don't see that there is anything else we can do," Ilse replied. "Not if we want to find your sister."

"What if we don't get anything back?" Gray asked.

"That is a chance we have to take."

3

"I still think I can find her without risking anything," Slania proposed.

"This way gives us double the chance," Ilse replied.

The past two hours had been spent in serious deliberation, each team member giving their opinion and debating the merits of every suggestion on the matter. A decision was finally reached, and they agreed to implement the plan.

Although not everyone was happy, they accepted the decision of the group as final.

Anja stared at Slania. "Have you come up with anything new?"

"No, ma'am."

"Then we don't have a choice."

The door to the ops room opened, and Mary Thurston walked in. "It looks like I got here just in time to stop you from doing something stupid."

Anja glared accusatorially at her team, her eyes burning into them. Thurston said, "Don't blame them. No one ratted you out. It was the next obvious step to take, and I knew you would all do it. So I hopped on a plane and flew out here."

The team remained silent.

"I am right, aren't I? You were about to release Lisa Bennett?"

Anja said, "It was my doing, nobody else's."

"Then, as I said, I'm glad I came. Going off and releasing a wanted felon is a criminal act. Possibly resulting in a prison sentence."

"Then you'd better lock us all up, General," Hawk said.

"I don't think so, Mr. Hawk. You will all stand down and go back to Santorini. Do I make myself clear?"

They all glared at her in silence.

"I cannot hear you?"

"Whatever," Hawk growled defiantly, getting to his feet. "It's fucking bullshit, is what it is."

Then he stormed out of the room.

"Jake, wait," Ilse called after him.

"Let him go," Thurston said. "He'll calm down."

"We have a chance to get Anja's sister back, and you want us to sit with our thumbs up our asses," Ilse grumbled. "It's wrong."

Thurston nodded. "Anyone else got something to say?"

"No, they haven't," Anja replied before anyone else could speak. "There is a chain of command, and they have been given their orders. Will there be anything else, General?"

"Not at this time."

"Then everyone is dismissed. Prepare to fly back to Santorini."

———

Lyon, France

The M7 in Lyon, France, ran along the Rhone River and at that time of night, was virtually deserted. The prisoner transfer truck moved steadily along the smooth surface, orange streetlamps flashing across the windshield like an external disco ball from the seventies.

The driver and passenger each checked their mirrors, noticing the headlights of a delivery truck pulling in behind them, matching their pace. They glanced at each other and kept on driving.

They had traveled another half mile when the delivery truck pulled out from behind them and began to overtake. The passenger grabbed his weapon as the vehicle drew level. Glancing across the lane at it, they noticed two people in the front.

Then the driver pushed his foot down farther, and it began pulling ahead of them.

"Whoa, shit!" the driver blurted out as the truck suddenly swerved and stopped in front of them.

The driver of the prisoner transport vehicle stomped on the brakes, and the tires chirped as it shuddered to a stop. Four people appeared from the truck in front, all armed with various weapons, walking toward the transport vehicle. The driver grabbed his weapon, but before he could do anything, the passenger pointed his gun at the man's head. "Just sit tight and it'll be over soon."

The driver froze and watched three of the people from the truck walk around the back. Inside the cab, the passenger flicked a switch which allowed the trio access. The fourth opened the driver's door and dragged him clear of the vehicle.

Within moments, the driver was bound and gagged and face down on the road.

A loud bang echoed in the confined space of the rear of the transport, and moments later, the three masked figures reappeared with a prisoner in tow, a woman, showing the effects of the stun grenade, with a hood over her head.

She was bundled into the back of the delivery truck, three masked people joining her. The fourth figure climbed behind the wheel of the truck while the guard from the transport sat in the passenger's seat.

The driver removed his mask and looked at the other man. "That went smoothly, boss."

Ian Groves nodded. "Yes, it did."

CHAPTER ONE

Singapore

"HERE WE GO AGAIN," Ilse Geller muttered as she monitored the screens in front of her. Removing her headset, she ran an exasperated hand through her mousey-colored hair. She put the headset back on and growled, "Jake, what the fuck are you doing?"

"Trying to get away from the bad guys, boss," came Hawk's reply.

In fact, Hawk was telling the truth. Close behind him came four armed men, firing guns at him from the darkness.

Jacob Hawk, former SAS soldier and Talon's premier field operative, stood at an imposing six feet four inches. His rugged face bore the evidence of countless missions, the scruff of a man who lived on the edge. In his early thirties, he carried the weight of experience, a shadow that clung to him like the memories he couldn't shake.

Ilse shared the same age bracket. She, too, had walked the treacherous path of the intelligence world. Ilse possessed a unique blend of resilience and recklessness.

Her movements betrayed the muscle memory of combat training, while her brown eyes had seen more than any woman her age should.

Their boss, Anja Meyer, was a former German intelligence commanding officer who navigated the murky waters of espionage with precision.

"You're on a billion-dollar golf course, Jake."

"Hence the motorized bloody golf buggy," Hawk snapped.

"Stop stuffing around."

"At least it wasn't an expensive car, blast your eyes."

"You haven't finished yet."

Suddenly, a large water hazard loomed out of the darkness in front of him. "Oh, shit!" Hawk exclaimed and threw himself from the buggy.

He rolled twice and came up holding his SIG Sauer P320. Meanwhile, the golf buggy disappeared into the murky depths.

He walked forward, in the direction of the pursuers as they came out of the darkness. The P320 fired. And fired. And fired.

Hawk rattled off half a magazine from the weapon, and by the time he was finished, three men were dead, and one was wounded. He grabbed the wounded man and growled, "Who sent you?"

The dying man coughed.

"Who fucking sent you?" Hawk snapped, trying again.

"F—Fox," the man gurgled before his body spasmed, then relaxed in death, leaving Hawk's hand holding a corpse.

"Shit. Alpha Two, did you get that?"

"Copy, Jake, I've got Slania running all we have. Are you all right?"

"Roger that. I'm moving to extract. See you there."

He broke into a jog across the dew-kissed dark expanse of the golf course, his breaths punctuated by the rhythm of his footsteps. The boundary loomed ahead, a low chain-link fence that marked the edge of the manicured course. With a swift leap, he cleared the obstacle, landing on the other side.

The van was ahead of him. Its windows reflected the moonlight, and the metal surface seemed to absorb the ambient sounds of the city. He approached, heart racing, and tugged at the van's sliding door. It yielded with a reluctant screech, revealing the dimly lit interior.

Slania sat there, hunched over her laptop, fingers dancing across the keyboard. The determination etched into her features showed how much concentration was going into it. She looked up as he climbed in, fatigue taking over. Without a word, she shook her head.

The van's engine came to life, and they merged into the flow of traffic. The darkness swallowed them, the streets winding like veins through the city's heart. Hawk glanced at Slania, who was staring at him again.

"What?" Hawk asked.

"You're fucking hopeless. Good thing the boss is in Yemen with Marcus otherwise she'd have your balls."

"The stand-in boss still might yet," Ilse growled as she put her foot on the gas pedal. "What the fuck, Jake?"

"I got a name," Hawk said.

"Yeah, but what the hell does it mean and why was he after us?"

"That's not in my department."

They'd come to Singapore running down a lead on a trafficker selling Asian girls to a smuggler likely shipping them to Russia and other countries in Eastern Europe. The name they had was Cuthbert.

The pertinence of *Fox* was new to them.

Cuthbert, on the other hand, happened to be Shakir

9

Ramli. A wealthy entrepreneur who lived a playboy life-style. Hawk had been surveilling the man when the four others had suddenly appeared.

Then they'd opened fire, trying to kill him. And they didn't know why.

———

SLANIA ALBRING WAS former Special Forces Group out of Belgium. But after three years there, had been picked for intelligence. She had long dark hair and a narrow face. Her build was slim, but rock-hard. What made her stand out was the tattoos covering a good portion of her body. Upon first glance, Anja's reaction had been, "She looks like the roof of the Sistine Chapel."

But beneath that colorful surface, Slania was one of the best in her field. She was about to discover something which would either be good, or open the door on another dangerous journey into the dark underbelly of the world of organized crime.

"I've got a hit on Fox," she said to Ilse.

"Already?" She seemed surprised. "That was fast."

"There is only one Fox coming up that rings alarm bells. Also known as the *Silver Fox*."

"A name? Facial?"

"No."

"Save it until Jake gets back. We'll run through it then. Are there any ties to Ramli?"

"Not that I can find. There must be something, though. Hence the hit squad."

"We need Ramli."

"I would say so, ma'am."

"Jake, can you hear me?"

"I sure can," Hawk replied.

"You need to secure Ramli as fast as possible. Your Fox friend is trying to kill him, and we need answers."

"Do you know where he is?" Hawk asked.

Ilse looked at Slania. She tapped a few keys. "His mansion."

"His mansion, Jake."

"Bloody miles away. How do you expect me to make it in time?"

"You're at a billion-dollar golf course, Jake. Do what you're good at. Steal a fast car."

She imagined his smile when he said, "I love it when you talk dirty to me."

"Don't fucking tell Anja."

THE MCLAREN 765LT rolled to a stop, and Hawk cut the motor. "Slania, can you get me through this gate?"

"Working on it. By the way, the car you stole belongs to Faris Swandi, the Godfather of organized crime on Singapore Island."

"I guess I'm off his Christmas card list this year then," Hawk said.

"Probably use your balls as a decoration on his tree," she replied.

The gate in front of Hawk slid open, and he heard Slania say, "I don't know why people make things so easy."

Starting the McLaren, Hawk drove through the gateway and up to the turnaround. Coming to a stop, he froze behind the wheel. "I've got two black SUVs on-site, and it looks like two guards are dead on the front steps."

Hawk waited for the driver's door to lift before climbing out. His P320 came up, and he said, "Yes, we definitely have a problem."

"Jake, you don't have to do this."

"Yes, I do."

Starting to move up the steps he stopped at the top near the door. "Slania, is there any way you can see inside?"

"Sorry, Jake, you're on your own."

Hawk chuckled grimly. "You have to love playing Robinson Crusoe."

Hawk checked his surroundings for threats before bending to investigate the two downed men. As expected, they were both dead. He picked up a fallen handgun and tucked inside his pants. "I'm going inside."

"Good copy."

The former SAS operator moved through the partially opened door and came into contact right away. The P320 in his fist fired the instant he saw the sentry in the entry hall. The man grunted and collapsed to the floor.

Of the three shots Hawk fired, two had found their mark. The third slapped into the wood paneling behind the man with a loud bang. Hawk muttered a curse. The sound was too loud to be missed.

And it wasn't. He heard startled voices coming from a closed door to his front right. Things were about to really kick off.

"Alpha One, I'm about to have contact."

"Copy."

As the voices grew louder, and it became immediately obvious that they were Russian. As the door ahead of him started to open, Hawk put half a magazine through it and heard someone cry out in pain.

A gun-filled hand poked around the doorjamb and blasted wildly, the unsuppressed muzzle crashing loudly. Hawk moved to his left, firing as he went.

Hitting a closed door with his shoulder, he felt it jar his body. Inside were two more shooters standing over a man tied to a chair. Hawk fired four times, and both men fell onto the hardwood floor. Hawk paused. "Threat neutralized."

He moved forward, covering the figure on the chair. He circled around so he could see the face more clearly. "Alpha One, I've found our pigeon. His feathers are plucked."

"Damn it."

"What do you want me to do?"

"Have a look around, Jake. See what you can find."

Hawk's hands moved with practiced efficiency, rifling through the drawers and the imposing wood cabinet. The air in the room smelled of aged paper and old books, the atmosphere heavy with anticipation. His eyes scanned the contents and found a jumble of faded documents.

It was then he discovered something of use. A ledger. Its leather cover bore the scars of time, its pages marked from much use. Hawk flipped it open, revealing rows of meticulously recorded transactions. Names, dates, numbers. He traced his finger along the entries, trying to decipher what they meant.

Setting it aside, he decided not to waste any more time on it now. He'd take it with him when he left.

But his mission demanded more. Hawk's fingers found a thumb drive, its innocuous appearance belied its significance. He dropped it into his pocket. Who knew what was on it.

Looking at Ramli, he asked, "Where do you hide all the good stuff, Cuthbert?"

The dead man said nothing.

Hawk let his eyes drift around the room, coming to rest on a large painting of a ship. A galleon. He glanced back at Ramli and said, "Is there gold behind that?"

Crossing the room to the painting, he pulled on one side and the catch released with an audible snick.

Hawk let it swing, revealing a large wall safe. "Slania, copy?"

"I'm here, Jake."

"I'm staring at a large safe. Electronic keypad with a fingerprint pad. Suggestions?"

"Brand?"

"Murray and Murray."

"Give me a moment."

"Take your time. It's not like I'm in the middle of a kill zone."

"Don't be a baby."

He continued his search while Slania did her thing. A couple of minutes later, she said, "I can give you a code that will override the locking system, but you will still need the fingerprint."

Hawk looked over at the dead man. "I can do that."

He freed Ramli and dragged his dead weight over to the safe. "All right, talk to me."

Slania read out the code. The pad beeped and asked for a fingerprint. Hawk pressed the right index finger against the reader, and nothing happened. "Shit."

"What's wrong."

"Not that finger."

"Try another. You've got nine left."

"You'll have to get lucky," Ilse said. "You've got three SUVs five mikes out."

"Shit. Give me that code again."

Slania rattled off the numbers. Nothing happened.

"Fuck, it has reset," Hawk hissed.

"Get out, Jake."

"Can you get me another code?"

"Damn it."

A moment later, she rattled off another. The pad beeped, and Hawk tried a different finger. Still nothing.

"I need another."

"Get out, Jake."

"Give me one more."

The code worked, and Hawk tried yet again."

"Three mikes, Jake," Ilse said impatiently.

"Got it."

The heavy door to the safe swung open smoothly, revealing a whole mass of thumb drives, not just the single one from before. Hawk stuffed them into his pocket and turned away before pausing and turning back. His eyes settled on the wads of cash just sitting there asking to be taken. Hawk said, "You are not a thief, Jake. Yeah, but I am a charity case."

He grabbed a few bundles and stuffed them into his shirt. "Time to go."

Hawk sprinted toward the front door, adrenaline surging through his veins. The distant hum of engines signaled danger closing in. His breaths came in ragged bursts as he reached the sleek silhouette of the McLaren, its metallic curves promising speed and escape.

Headlights sliced through the darkness, illuminating the gravel driveway. Bullets erupted, their staccato rhythm shattering the night. Metal met metal as they ricocheted off the McLaren's chassis. Hawk flung himself into the driver's seat, heart pounding. The engine roared to life, a symphony of power and desperation.

Hawk put it in gear and floored the gas pedal, swinging hard on the wheel. The rear end flicked around and before he knew it, the McLaren rocketed back along the drive with bullets chasing it.

The SUVs spun around and gave chase.

And they were fast. Porsche Turbo with a top speed of almost 200 MPH. The McLaren peaked at around 205 MPH.

Fast cars on Singapore streets. What could possibly go wrong?

The McLaren handled well, but for some reason, at high speed it was scary. Besides, the narrow street he was currently on was potholed and uneven. The SUVs, however, seemed to get a better ride and had closed the gap on their target.

An intersection came up fast, a red light screaming at Hawk to stop. But it was the middle of the night. No one would be—

"Fuck!" Hawk blurted as he narrowly avoided a small Hyundai cutting across the intersection in front of him.

His foot came off the gas automatically, and the McLaren slowed. Then, once he had composed himself, the pedal went down again.

"Jake, are you all right?" Slania asked.

"That was close."

"Yes, I saw it."

"Any ideas?" Hawk asked as he slowed for an upcoming turn. The intersection was on him faster than he figured, and he was forced to stand hard on the brakes. He turned right and gave the vehicle a solid feed of gas.

WHAP! WHAP! WHAP! Bullets hammered the thin exterior of the McLaren.

"Why do assholes like shooting bloody huge craters in nice cars?" Hawk asked.

"Possibly for the same reason assholes like stealing them," Ilse replied.

"That's not nice," he retorted.

"Turn left, Jake."

Standing on the brakes once more, the tires chirped in protest. He missed the turn. "Here we go again. You have to tell me about the bloody turns before I get there."

"I thought you could drive," Slania replied. "Take the exit on your left in two hundred meters."

"Where will that take me?"

"Pan-Island Expressway."

Hawk nodded. "Good, that'll sort out the men from the boys."

"Ah, Jake..." Ilse started.

"What?"

"You know how when things seem about to work out all right and something happens?"

He took the exit up onto the expressway. "Yes."

"Well..."

"It's a bloody helicopter, isn't it?" he growled. "It's always a bastard fucking helicopter."

"Maybe."

"Man, I hate this job. I think I'll bloody retire. Shit. Where is it?" The helicopter screamed low overhead, the downdraft buffeting the McLaren. "Don't bother. I can see it. Makes me wish I'd gone to bloody Yemen."

The helicopter seemed to turn on a dime in midair. It pointed its nose down at the speeding McLaren and opened fire. The asphalt on the expressway appeared to take on a life of its own eruptions coming toward him as the rounds impacting it grew closer in the orange light of the streetlamps. Hawk swung hard on the wheel, and the speeding vehicle responded immediately. It swerved around the twin lines of death approaching him and was soon clear.

With the McLaren back under control, Hawk pressed the gas pedal down even further. The vehicle shot forward and opened a larger gap from the pursuing SUVs.

But he couldn't outrun the helicopter.

"Jake, the helicopter is coming back around."

"Your point is?" Hawk asked Ilse in frustration.

She was about to reply when the MH-6 opened fire. The rear of the McLaren was hit, and it kicked out wildly. Hawk felt it going, but there was nothing he could do about it.

Then the car flipped and started rolling crazily.

Components flew into the air before the vehicle slid along on its roof and came to a halt in the middle of the expressway.

The pursuing SUVs braked hard and came to a halt. The occupants climbed out and approached the wrecked McLaren, their weapons ready to fire.

As they surrounded it, the leader bent and looked inside. The vehicle was empty. There was no sign of the driver anywhere.

CHAPTER TWO

Yemen.

YEMEN WAS HOT, and Anja hated it. Marcus Gray, on the other hand, seemed to be at home in the heat. Trying and blend in and maintain their cover, the pair was dressed like locals. Unlike most of the locals, they were armed with AKs and had spare ammunition tucked beneath their robes. Against their skin they wore their Synoprathetic suits. The way the country was at that time, they fit right in, however, Anja's face was covered because women were required to do so.

The Land Rover bumped over several deep ruts, unable to avoid hitting them. Somewhere ahead was Lisa Bennett. She had a meeting with one of her customers in the country.

"Sorry, boss," Marcus Gray said. A former para, he had five years' experience in one combat zone or another. In his late twenties, Gray looked younger than his age, and his face and head were covered in thick, dark hair. And like Hawk, he was dependable in hairy situations.

Anja, on the other hand, was athletic with a thin face,

although smudged with Yemeni dust, and in her mid-thirties. Her head covering concealed the blonde hair beneath. She'd been in command of Talon since their inception and would walk through the fires of hell for any of her people. She looked down at the screen in her lap. The signal from the tracker that had been implanted in Lisa Bennett when the mission was set up was still strong.

Her sister was out here in this God-forsaken land somewhere and they had to find her.

In one of Russia's many political prisons, Marlene had been incarcerated there until being purchased by Lisa Bennett and then transported out here, along with many others, the purpose of which was to provide war brides for Yemeni fighters.

On standby were two Chinook helicopters with a Global Strike Team on board each. ST Falcon, and ST Mongoose. One call, and they were in.

This was why Anja believed her career, once this mission was done, would be over. To get the teams, she'd had to confess her sins to Mary Thurston.

––––––––

One Week Previous, Lyon, France

Ian Groves and Helen Smith escorted a hooded Lisa Bennett into an empty warehouse. A lone chair sat in the middle of the dusty concrete floor, a bright floodlight above it, dust motes dancing in its rays. They pushed her into the chair and then disappeared into the darkness once dismissed with a nod of Anja's head.

Standing beside Anja were Hawk and Ilse. All were armed and knew the consequences of what they had just orchestrated: career-ending for them.

"Do it," Anja said.

Hawk took a few steps forward and removed the hood. In her mid-twenties, Bennett's dark hair was disheveled from the hood being ripped off. Lisa blinked and looked around to get her bearings. When she recognized her captors, she gave the three a look of disdain. "I thought I was rid of you pathetic people."

Anja stared at her, ignoring the jibe. "This is a one-time deal, Lisa. Take it or leave it, but know that this may be your final opportunity to ever see freedom again."

Lisa's face remained impassive. Being locked in a cell for the rest of her life wasn't her definition of ideal. "I'm listening."

"I'm going to release you. You will have two days to gather all the intel you can and find the whereabouts of my sister. You will then return here for further instructions. Understood?"

"What if I don't?"

"Then you go to prison."

"No, what if I don't come back?"

"That would be a grave error on your part," Anja replied.

"What? I go to prison?" There was sarcasm in her voice.

"No, we will find you and kill you."

The look on Anja's face showed the veracity of her words, and there was no doubt in Lisa's mind as she stared at her. She nodded slowly. "There has to be something in it for me."

"You will be released."

Lisa Bennett grinned wryly. "I must be hearing things. For a moment, I thought you said you were going to let me go."

"That's right."

"Then I guess I'll do it."

"Remember what I said," Anja warned her. *"And I do keep my promises."*

———

TWO DAYS LATER, Lisa Bennett returned to the same warehouse. *"I know where she is."*

"Where?"

"Yemen."

"Where in Yemen?"

"Get me a map."

Hawk produced a map and held it against the metal wall. Bennett ran her finger over it, locating the position as she pointed at a stretch of desert in Hadramout Province. *"There used to be a town here. Now, it's more rubble than anything. Mostly caused by airstrikes. It is occupied by a force of AQAP fighters. The women will be there."*

Anja felt anger surge through her, and Hawk knew she was about to explode. He said, *"Is she there?"*

"As far as I could ascertain."

"The buyer, is he there too?"

"Yes."

Hawk nodded. *"Good, set up a meeting with him."*

Lisa's jaw dropped. *"What?"*

"Set up a meeting with him."

"No. I've done my bit. I'm not—"

Hawk's eyes narrowed. *"Your bit is done when we fucking say so. Set up the meeting."*

Although reluctantly, she did just that.

The next part of the operation involved Mary Thurston.

"You know there is no coming back from this, Anja, don't you?" Thurston asked her from the other end of the video call in Hereford.

"I knew that before I started, ma'am. The others had no

involvement in this at all, and I would like that put on the record."

"The fuck we didn't," Hawk snapped as he stepped in beside his boss. "Boss, I was in this up to my bloody eyeballs."

"Me too," Ilse said as she joined them.

"Me too, ma'am," Slania said.

"Ah shit, what the hell," Marcus growled. "Might as well fire us all, ma'am."

Mary Thurston stared at them. Dressed casually in her usual jeans and jumper, she wanted nothing to do with suits or formal attire. Her dark hair was out, falling past her shoulders. She sighed. "I should throw the damn book at you and lock you up in a deep dark hole. But we don't have a book, and the weather is too fucking lousy to dig a hole. Tell me the plan."

"Ilse, Jacob, and Slania will work a lead we've been investigating, while Marcus and I will head to Yemen. Lisa Bennett will be injected with a tracking device so we can follow at a safe distance. All we need is a couple of Strike Teams, ma'am. Oh, and a couple of Chinooks."

"You will need overwatch."

"Yes, ma'am."

Another sigh. "Fine. We shall continue this once you return and your sister is safe. Understood?"

"Yes, ma'am."

The call ended, and Anja turned to her people. "Thank you."

"You would have done the same for us, boss," Hawk said with a grin.

"I've never felt prouder of this team than I do right now. When this is over, I will do whatever it takes to save your jobs."

"Let's just get your sister back first," Ilse said. "Then we'll worry about our jobs."

Yemen

"The town shouldn't be far away," Anja said to Gray.

"I hope not, boss, I've had enough of this bloody goat track."

"Sparrow One, this is Nightingale, copy? Over."

"Read you Lima Charlie, Nightingale. Send traffic."

"One, ISR has the target rather busy. Maybe thirty to forty fighting-age males on the ground."

Global had also supplied a UCAV to provide air cover in case they needed it before the strike teams arrived.

"Good copy, Nightingale. Progress on Ferret?"

"Ferret is coming up on target now. Have a good visual on her. Suggest you circle the town and come in from the east on foot. Will direct you to the meet from above."

"Roger that, Nightingale. One out." Anja looked at Gray. "Did you get that?"

"Yes, boss."

"Do it."

———

WITH A RAISED HEART RATE, Lisa Bennett's nerves tightened like a noose as she drove toward the desolate town. The remnants of bombed-out buildings loomed ahead, their skeletal frames a grim testament to past violence. But these ruins were no mere relics—they had been repurposed by the terrorists into an impregnable fortress.

At the perimeter, Lisa's pulse quickened further. The checkpoint was her gateway, guarded by vigilant eyes. Anja's parting gift to her was a Glock with a single magazine.

Above, the UCAV—Unmanned Combat Aerial Vehicle—patrolled, its unblinking eye tracking her every move. Lisa knew its capabilities, advanced surveillance, and voice recording technology. Her words would be scrutinized, dissected by unseen ears. She swallowed, her mouth dry, and wondered what the immediate future held.

The Land Cruiser rolled to a stop and three armed men walked toward her. Lisa gripped the Glock out of sight and waited. One of the men, unshaven, a wild look in his eyes, pointed his AK at her and said, "Speak or I will kill you."

"I—I am Lisa Bennett. I'm here to see Jambiya."

"Why would a western whore be here to see our great leader?" the terrorist sneered.

"This whore is the one who would kill you if you don't do as I say," Lisa growled.

Anger flared in the man, and he reached for the door handle. However, his hand had only just touched the hot surface when the Glock appeared, and the gaping hole of its muzzle winked at the stunned terrorist. "Do as I ask."

The man could do nothing except what he was asked. "Leave the vehicle here and follow me."

Lisa turned off the motor and climbed out into the heat of the day. The terrorist turned away and started to walk. Lisa began to follow him, then everything went black.

———

"SHE'S DOWN, Ferret is down. Someone just hit her from behind."

"Damn it, Nightingale, tell me what is happening," Anja said, as the Land Rover skidded through a deep furrow in the gravel road.

"Not sure at this time, One. She got out of the vehicle to follow one of the males and was hit from behind. They're now carrying her into the town."

"Damn it. Keep me updated. Out." Ilse bashed the dash with her hand. "Fuck it. Get off here, Marcus. We can't risk getting too close to the town."

Gray pulled the Land Rover off the road and parked in a gully. They climbed out and crawled up a low rise to where they could observe the town itself. Anja took out her binoculars and scanned the ruins. "It's hard to see much from here."

Gray said, "It looks like this gully circles around close to the town, boss. We could use it for cover to get closer."

Anja nodded. "Let's do it. Nightingale, this is One. We're proceeding to target on foot. Have Falcon and Mongoose stand by."

"Copy. One is proceeding on foot."

The heat in the gully was stifling but every step they took led them closer to the town. From somewhere within the ruined fortress, they could hear automatic weapons fire rattling across the rubble. Once past the outskirts, they moved into the town.

Some buildings were still standing, although they were few and far between. Most had been brought down, the result of multiple air strikes. Gray led the way through the rubble. "Two, hold position."

The warning was calm.

"Sitrep, Nightingale?"

"Two, you have an X-ray coming your way. Twenty meters out should appear shortly." Gray took out his suppressed Glock and pressed his back against what remained of the wall where they were hiding.

A few moments later, he heard approaching footsteps. Gray waited patiently for the sound to get closer, like a sonar pinging a submarine. Then, when the sound was almost on top of him, the former para stepped out and shot the man. Twice in the chest, once in the head. The terrorist dropped to the ground, and Gray immediately dragged him into cover.

Slinging the AK, Gray stayed on point. "Nightingale, this is Two. Sitrep?"

"They have Feret in the center of town. It appears to be the old town square. Keep moving. When you get there, you will see a half-demoed building. It should provide you with cover and overwatch."

"Roger that."

Gray pushed on. Anja walked behind him, turning occasionally to check their six. They kept to cover as best they could until reaching the building that Nightingale had described.

The interior was like a hollowed-out shell. It must have taken a direct hit from a bomb. The floor above had a ragged hole through it. The staircase leading upward was missing a small section which they had to climb across.

Once at the top, they crept over to a jagged hole in the wall where a window would once have been. Peering out at the square, they saw the gathering crowd below. At its center was Lisa Bennett, on her knees, head bowed.

"This can't be good," Gray said.

"No, not in the slightest."

———

THE PAIN in her head was roaring like a train. Lisa looked up from where she was on her knees and said, "I'm here to see Jambiya."

A tall, thin terrorist stepped in closer and punched her in the face. Lisa's mouth filled with blood, and she rocked to one side. She spat blood and looked up. "Jambiya."

He hit her again. Harder this time and she fell into the

27

dirt. Blood running from her mouth, Lisa spat more out onto the dry earth. She forced herself back to her knees and said, "Jambiya, fucking asshole."

The fist came back again.

"Stop." The voice was calm, almost soothing. "What is going on?"

"The western whore says she is here to see you, Exalted One," the terrorist said.

"Her?" He seemed surprised. "Who are you, woman?"

"Lisa Bennett."

"You? You are Lisa Bennett, who sells the women?"

"Yes."

"I thought you would be older."

"Not hardly."

"Why are you here?" Jambiya asked.

"I need a place to hide for a while," Lisa said.

"Hide? From whom?"

"I escaped from British Intelligence. I need to hide."

Jambiya stared at her. "British Intelligence is after you and this is where you come?"

"Yes," Lisa replied. She looked around. "Where are all the women? I will stay with them."

Instinctively, Jambiya pointed toward a damaged building over his shoulder. "They are in there. That is where they stay until we want them. When we don't want them anymore, we kill them."

Her blood ran cold at the look in his eyes. Not for the deaths of the women she had sold into this life, but because, for the first time, she realized that this was a one-way ticket. The feeling was confirmed when Jambiya took out his handgun and shot her in the head.

———

"FUCK, HIT HIM," Anja snarled. "Nightingale this is One. Launch the QRF now. I say again, launch now."

"Roger that, launching QRF."

While she was making the call, Gray sighted on Jambiya with his AK and squeezed the trigger. The side of the killer's head blew out with the single 7.62 round that punched through bone and brain.

Gray shifted his aim and dropped another terrorist who stood there stunned. A third who turned to run took one step before another AK round ruined his day.

Anja joined the fight as a couple of the terrorist men commenced a steady rate of fire back at their position. Bullets chipped concrete away from decimated walls as they ricocheted away harmlessly. Anja picked out a target and shot him in the chest.

He flopped back, jerking crazily, releasing the grip on his weapon. Beside him on the dirt was a shooter that Gray had just killed.

Now, the square below them was clear except for the dead. The remaining terrorists had taken up positions throughout the rubble and were getting down to business.

"Sparrow One, this is Strike Lead, how copy?"

"Good copy, Strike Lead," Anja returned.

"I need a sitrep on target."

"You need to put down outside of the town and work toward us, copy?"

"Roger that. Strike Lead is three mikes out. Be with you directly."

Gray selected a target in the mounds of rubble but was having a hard time hitting him. The shooter was like a jackrabbit bobbing up and down. So, he timed the bob.

Pulled the trigger.

Terrorist dead.

Beside him, Anja's AK rattled out its staccato beat.

After a moment, she dropped out the magazine and reloaded.

Gray said, "You're burning too much ammo, boss."

"You bloody worry about what you're doing," she snapped at him.

"If you burn through it and the QRF can't get in, then we're a weapon down. Sorry, boss, but slow your fucking roll."

She knew he was right and adjusted accordingly.

"Sparrow One, this is Strike Lead. Strike Two is putting down now, we're going to make a run to take the heat off."

"Copy, Strike Lead."

At first, they heard nothing, then the booming whop-whop of helicopter blades and the roar of engines seemed to buffet them physically. The rear ramp was down, and a couple of the strike team members were firing through the opening. Anja suddenly felt relaxed at the sight of the Chinook, but it didn't last. What happened next shattered that.

"RPG!" Gray shouted into his comms. "Pull up. Pull up."

But it was too late. The big beast started to move up and away, but the rocket-propelled grenade was already on top of it. But as luck would have it, the body of the heli-copter was spared a direct impact, only the front rotor blades were hit.

The Chinook tipped and fell onto its side, the rear rotor blades shattering on impact. "Oh, no," Anja gasped.

"Strike Two, Strike Lead is down, I say again, Strike Lead is down. You need to double-time it in here, mate."

"Copy, Two. We're on our way."

Normally, a Strike team would consist of 4-5 opera-tors. This time, they had gone in heavy with eight per team. Strike Team Mongoose was on the downed chopper. Falcon was already on the ground.

"Cover me," Gray said and jumped to his feet.

"Where are you going, Marcus?"

"To help out."

He disappeared and Anja started shooting again, this time spacing her shots. As figures began to emerge from the downed helicopter, they took up position and started to defend the crash site. "Mongoose One, this is Sparrow One, copy?"

"Copy, Sparrow."

"Sitrep."

"Unclear, Sparrow. Will advise."

"Roger that. Falcon is on the way in."

"Tell Geordie to hurry up, boss."

"Copy. Falcon One, this is Sparrow. Sitrep."

"Almost there, boss."

Suddenly, down below, Gray appeared, laying down fire as he approached the downed helicopter. He crouched beside the Mongoose team leader, and they talked momentarily. Then he came over Anja's comms. "Boss, we've got two injured in the heli."

"Copy."

The sudden increase in gunfire indicated to Anja that the other team had arrived. She watched as they started to methodically clear areas and drive the terrorists back. Before long, the area was clear, and the operators were mopping up. Anja came down and found Gray.

"How are the injured?"

"They'll be fine. Broken leg, another was knocked out and has a concussion."

"We have to find the women," she told him.

"We'll have a look around, boss."

Anja looked at the supine form of Lisa Bennett. Her

sightless eyes were open, looking up at the cloudless sky. "I didn't want her dead."

"Saves a lot of hassle that way, boss," Gray said. "A lot of people safer in the world, too."

Anja stared at Gray in silence before nodding slowly. "Yes, you're right."

"Ma'am, over here," one of the strike team operators called over to her. He was standing next to the structure that the terrorist leader had been pointing to.

Anja and Gray walked toward him. He stepped back away from the doorway as figures began to emerge. At first, it was just a couple but then it turned into six, then eight, then ten. They were dressed from head to foot, faces covered. Anja gasped.

Slinging her weapon, she hurried toward the women. "Marlene? Marlene Roth? Is Marlene Roth here?"

A figure stopped in front of Anja and took off her face cover. The woman looked gaunt, and there were dark rings around her eyes. "Anja?"

"Marlene?"

"Yes, it's me."

"Oh, good Lord," Anja gasped and wrapped her arms around her sister. "I can't believe it. I just can't. After all this time, to find you are safe. Don't worry, we will take you home."

"That would be good," Marlene whispered in her sister's ear. That would be good."

CHAPTER THREE

Santorini Island, Greece

ANJA ROLLED OFF GRAY, and they lay side-by-side, sweat glistening on their naked bodies, the ceiling fan stirring the air above them. This was a first and it had come out of the blue, totally unexpected. Gray figured that if the others had been at the villa, it never would have happened. But the tension of the newly completed mission, a few relaxing beers, and the enjoyment of each other's company had contributed to the melding of bodies.

"Your sister okay, boss?" Gray asked tentatively.

"You don't have to make small talk, Marcus," Anja said.

"Sorry."

"Don't be. She is fine. She is in London at the Global Medical Facility. I'll head over next week and visit with her."

"She was lucky."

"Damn lucky."

Anja got off the bed, walked over to the double glass sliding doors and looked out over the swimming pool area.

It was late in the afternoon, and the sun was on its way down. Gray studied her from behind. The muscles in her back were well-defined, like the rest of her body. Many hours in the villa gym saw to that.

She turned and stared at Gray. "Come and swim with me, Marcus."

"Yes, ma'am."

"Don't call me ma'am, or boss, or whatever else you think you should. I have a name."

"Yes, ma'am—Anja." He followed her out into the pool, the cool water wrapping him in its wet embrace. "Are you sure the others will be back tomorrow?"

"Yes. Then we have another mission to plan for."

Gray swam over to Anja, who wrapped her arms around him and kissed his lips. She pulled away before saying, "Don't think that this will be a regular occurrence, Marcus. It's a one-off thing. Just two people releasing their built-up tension."

"Sure." He felt himself harden again. "Whatever you say."

Anja brought her legs up, trapping him between her thighs. Then she reached down and positioned him where she wanted before sliding down onto his shaft. They were soon both crying out in ecstasy once more, oblivious to all that surrounded them.

"I guess we shouldn't have come home early," a voice said from the side of the pool.

Anja and Gray turned their heads and looked at the three figures standing there. Hawk's grin widened. "I guess we're interrupting, boss."

Anja lowered her head so that it was nestled in the crook of Gray's neck. "Fuck!"

———

ANJA WAS WEARING jeans and a T-shirt when she walked into the large living room where the others were sitting and drinking beer. She glared at Hawk who was staring at her. "What are you looking at, Jacob?"

"Nothing, boss."

Ilse was beside Hawk and punched him in the thigh with a low growl. "Grow up, Jake. What they do is none of our business."

"Fine, fine," Hawk said.

Slania looked up from where she was peeling the sticker off her beer bottle. "That's shit. Everybody is getting some except for me."

"Can we just drop it," Anja snapped. "It happened, it's over. Move on."

"Yes, boss," Hawk replied.

Gray walked into the room. "What's happening?"

"We were just discussing your sex life and how Slania is like a desert."

"Fuck, Jake," Ilse snapped.

"Have you finished with Marcus, boss?"

"He's all yours."

Gray looked at Slania. "Don't look at me."

"Can we change the subject?" Ilse asked.

"Let's," Anja said. "Tell me, what mischief did Jacob get up to on the mission in Singapore?"

"You'd be proud of me, boss, I only stole a golf cart."

Anja raised her eyebrows and looked at a sticking plaster on his arm. "Really? So, was the McLaren 765LT a figment of your imagination?"

Hawk looked at Ilse. She shrugged. "What? It's all in the report."

"So, you would know that it was owned by a criminal, too, right?"

"Uh, huh. Okay, let's go over your mission."

"Wait," Ilse said. "How is your sister?"

"She is fine. Better than expected."

Ilse left it at that. "Okay. We have a name. The Silver Fox. I don't know who he is but Cuthbert was involved with him somehow. That was why he was trying to kill him."

Anja frowned. "I think I might have heard that name somewhere before. Though I can't place it."

"We got a few thumb drives from Ramli's safe, boss," Hawk said. "Slania has started going through them but hasn't come up with anything as yet."

"Keep at it tomorrow. Maybe something will pop."

"Boss."

"Anything else?"

"Whoever this Silver Fox is, he has a lot of money. Has to be a big organization," Ilse said. "To respond the way he did, in the manner he did, this is something big."

"Medusa big?" Anja asked.

"I hope not."

"Me too."

"Although it looks as though he has fingers in a few pies."

"Dig deep."

They spent the rest of the evening catching up. Later that evening while Ilse and Hawk were in bed, Hawk said, "Do you think it's been going on long?"

Ilse traced a finger down his hairy washboard stomach. "What?"

"Gray and the boss?"

Ilse groaned. "Let it go, Jake. Anyone would think you're jealous of them."

"Me? Not bloody likely. I've got my hands full with you, love. That's bad enough."

"Don't sound so happy," she fired back at him.

"Not what I meant."

There was a prolonged silence before Ilse said, "Jake, what would you do if I got pregnant?"

She heard his breath catch in his throat. "What kind of question is that?"

"What would you do?"

"Shit, you're not, are you."

"No, of course not. But I want to know. It could happen. We are sleeping together, and birth control isn't foolproof. Or Jake proof, for that matter."

"Honestly, I don't know."

"What do you mean?"

There was concern in her voice.

"I mean, I don't know. There would be a lot of things to weigh up. I mean, we don't exactly live in the safest of environments. Shit, I could get killed tomorrow. It would be a big thing. Would you keep it?"

"Yes." The word came out fast and definite.

"Would you stay with me if I kept working?" he asked.

"I don't know." Hawk expected the answer. He'd seen so many relationships stretched to breaking point and then snap because of the lifestyle. Ilse said, "Are you saying you would stay with me?"

"Yes."

"That is why I love you, Jacob Hawk."

Hawk groaned. "How did we get onto this soppy shit?"

"It was your fault."

———

THE FOLLOWING MORNING, while Slania dug into the mountain of intel they'd acquired from Cuthbert, Ilse and Hawk went out to find a café and have coffee. It was good to get out and spend some quality time to themselves. Lately, while on missions, they'd been too preoccupied to make the time. But that was an agreement they made.

Hawk's coffee was standard. Black, no sugar. Ilse had a latte. As they sat and talked they were surrounded mostly by tourists doing the same as them. At one table, Hawk noticed a young couple nearby speaking French.

There were other couples, mainly older, and two men sitting on the outer fringe as well. It was these two that drew Hawk's attention. "Ilse, there are two blokes at our three. You see them?"

She looked at them then back at Hawk. "Sure, why?"

"There is something off about them."

"Oh, Jake. Can't you switch off?"

"Honestly, there is something about them."

"Sweetheart, stop. Can't we just enjoy the moment?"

He nodded. "Fine."

But as they drank and chatted, he kept one eye on them. Then, out of nowhere, he said, "They're military. Or were."

"You just want to ruin it, don't you?" Ilse growled. "The sun is out, it's a beautiful morning, and you just want to ruin it."

"No, I don't," he replied. "Some things just trigger me."

"How about I just ask them to join us?"

"Now you're being silly."

Ilse got up. "I'll see you at home."

"Wait, what are you doing?"

"I am going back to lay by the pool in that new white bikini I bought," she told him.

"I'd stay away from the pool if I were you. Especially after what we saw Marcus and the boss doing in it. It'll be full of tadpoles."

Ilse rolled her eyes and walked off. Hawk almost got to his feet and followed her, but something kept him there. It was ten minutes later that the French couple left after finishing their drinks. Hawk watched them walk away holding hands.

Then, the two men followed them.

Hawk's face grew serious. "All right, let's see what you blokes are up to."

He got to his feet and started to follow. The street they were on was narrow, not wide enough for a vehicle, which made it perfect for foot traffic. Staying back, he tailed the pair as they followed the French couple in front.

Losing sight of the men around the corner of a stark white building trimmed with royal blue, a sudden scream drew Hawk's attention.

"Shit," he growled and started running, taking out his P320 as he went.

No sooner had he turned the corner when he saw the young man lying on the hard street and the two men fighting with the young woman as they tried to bundle her into a van beside them.

"Shit. Hey! Assholes," Hawk called out. He brought his weapon up but didn't want to fire just in case he hit her.

One of the men turned and noticed Hawk in the middle of the street. He left his friend to deal with the woman, stepped away from the vehicle and brought out his own handgun.

"Don't," Hawk called a warning to him.

The man didn't listen and kept the weapon moving. "Motherfucker."

The P320 crashed twice, and the kidnapper jerked under the impact of the two rounds. He collapsed to the street, spasmed, then never moved again. Hawk walked forward, the weapon pointed in the direction of the second kidnapper. "Let her go, mate. I'll kill you if you don't."

He gave Hawk a confused look as he contemplated several outcomes. The Brit shook his head. "Be sensible, mate."

Then, with a snarl, he cast the woman aside and tried to pull his weapon. It was no contest. Hawk fired twice, and the man died.

The Brit shook his head. "Now I'm going to be in fucking trouble again."

————

The Urals

The man known as the Silver Fox stared out over the snow-covered landscape from the parapet of his own castle. He sipped his wine and turned back to the large room when he heard the noise behind him. A tall, slim, attractive woman approached him across the library's stone floor. Her long silver-blonde hair fell past her shoulders onto the silky fabric of her form-fitting red dress. He smiled at her. "Hello, my love. You look elegant this evening."

"Thank you, Father. I just came to see if you will be dining with me tonight. I do hate eating alone."

The Silver Fox smiled at his daughter. "Of course, nothing would give me greater pleasure, my dear."

She kissed him on the cheek. Stepping back, she looked into his eyes. "You seem troubled, Father."

He gave her a wan smile. "Just business, my love. Nothing to worry about."

"These mercenaries you were talking about?" she asked.

He nodded. "Yes."

"I will have someone keep an eye on them," his

daughter replied. "If need be, a team can be dispatched to make them go away."

He reached out and patted his daughter on the shoulder. "You are in the image of your father. I did not want this for you, but it seems that it has been taken out of my hands."

"It is the businesswoman in me."

"We will need to replace Cuthbert," the Silver Fox told his daughter.

"Already taken care of. We will be receiving another shipment of girls within the next two weeks. In the meantime, I have to leave for the west tomorrow."

"Will you be taking anyone with you?"

She nodded. "Just Vadim. Maybe my team."

Her father nodded his permission. "Good, good. Vadim is reliable. Now, shall we have that dinner?"

"Yes."

"I CAN'T BELIEVE you left me there for two days," Hawk growled as he and Anja walked toward the villa.

"For the hundredth time, Jake, I didn't leave you there. The police just work slower here."

"Do we know who they were?" he asked.

"Slania thinks they are French. Their names say so but she's trying to nail it down."

"Why come here? Do they know each other?" Hawk asked.

Anja shrugged. "Not that we can tell. As for your first question, sleepy holiday destination. Good place to kidnap some fresh meat."

When they reached the villa and went inside, they found Slania working diligently, attired only in a bikini top and shorts, while drinking a beer. She looked up and said, "How was the holiday?"

"Fine, thank you for asking."

"The boss could have left you there for longer. Ilse wanted her to."

Hawk glanced at Anja who shrugged. Then Ilse appeared. She glared at Hawk and walked out to the pool. "Looks like I'm in the shit."

Anja stared at her operations officer and said to Hawk, "Sort it out, just in case we have to go on a mission."

"Yes, ma'am."

He strolled out to the pool area and sat next to Ilse, who was dangling her feet in the water. "Hey."

"Hey yourself."

———

ANJA CROSSED the room to where Slania was working. "Have you found anything?"

"A couple of threads we might be able to pull," she replied. "Chasseurs."

"Hunters?"

"Yes. One of the dead men had it tattooed on his arm," Slania explained. "Alone, it was just another tattoo. But when I did a first scan through the drives that Jake took from Cuthbert, I came across the name again."

"Interesting. Did you tell Ilse?"

Slania nodded. "Yes, she was going to reach out to some of her contacts in France, and German intelligence."

"Chasseurs. It sounds like more than one person. Do we know if the other man had a tattoo the same?"

Slania looked through her papers. "Damn, I bloody missed it. He did."

"It's okay. So, we're looking at a group. Kidnap for hire," Anja said. "Ilse, can you come in here, please?"

Ilse kissed Hawk on the cheek and stood up. She shook the excess water from her feet and went inside. "What's up?"

"Slania overlooked something which she has just rectified. The Chasseurs."

"That's right, the tattoo."

"Both of the kidnappers had one."

Ilse raised her eyebrows. "An organization?"

"Could be."

Hawk appeared. "Intel meeting?"

"In a way," Anja said and told him what they had found.

"Great, another kidnap-for-hire bunch." Hawk looked around. "Where is Marcus?"

"I'm not sure."

"It would appear that we're going to France," Hawk said.

"We may well be, just give it time. Slania and Ilse are still working the problem. Once we have more, then we will make plans."

"What about this Silver Fox name?"

"Still just that," Ilse said. "Only a name."

"All right, in that case, who wants a beer?"

They all raised their hands.

———

GRAY TURNED UP AN HOUR LATER, walking out to the pool then sat down with a beer. Hawk was reading a book nearby and glanced at his friend. "Hey, Casanova."

"Fuck off, Jake."

Hawk frowned and put the book down. "Whoa, what's up?"

"Just not in the mood for your shit."

"Okay, sorry I spoke, but now spill."

43

"I keep thinking about the boss."

"You do, or that slug between your legs?" Hawk asked.

"It was a mistake and now I can't stop thinking about it. Shit."

"Has it happened again?" he asked Gray.

"No."

"Then forget about it. She probably has done. She needed a release, and you were it."

"But—"

"But what?"

"She's fucking hot."

Hawk grinned. "That's your dick talking, son. Forget about it."

"Easy for you to say, you have Ilse," he pointed out.

"I tried to discourage her. Look, if you need to get over her, go and bang Slania. She'll—"

"She'll what?" Slania asked as she came out to the pool area.

"Marcus needs a fuck to get over the boss," Hawk said. "She's screwed his brain."

Slania glared at him. "What? So, you chose me? Asshole."

"Why not? You're hot. Single. And you were complaining about getting none."

"Shit Jake, you're a fucking neanderthal," Slania growled.

Out of the corner of his eye, Hawk caught Gray grinning. "Well, at least you're smiling, now."

Slania stared at the former para. "Shit, if you need a pity fuck, Marcus, I'll help you out."

Hawk nodded. "See, I told you. Slania is kind, too."

"You won't think so after I tell Ilse what you said," Slania told him.

"Tell Ilse what?"

Hawk looked up at his partner. "Ah fuck it."

CHAPTER FOUR

Santorini Island, Greece

"DON'T YOU EVER SLEEP?" Hawk asked Slania later that night when he emerged for a glass of water.

"I could say the same about you, Jake," she replied. "Where is Ilse?"

"In the land of nod," he said, meaning asleep. "Hey, I'm sorry about earlier."

"Don't worry about it," Slania said with a grin. "I happen to like Marcus, and I would help him out if he needed it."

"He needs something to get over the boss."

Slania turned her head to look at him. "Maybe he already had something."

Hawk grinned. "Damn. I hope the silly pillock doesn't get hung up on you, now. No offense."

"I'm sure he will be fine. Besides, I enjoy eating grass both sides of the fence."

Hawk's grin broadened. "I like that."

"Don't think I'm going to be nice to you all the time, Jake."

"Wouldn't have it any other way. Have you found anything?"

Slania hit a few keys, and a picture popped up. "This is Marcel Blanc. By day, he is an advertising executive, and by night, he lives on the dark web as an intermediary, or middleman to the uneducated, setting up services for persons with certain needs. If anyone knows about the Chasseurs, it will be him."

"Then it's him we need to talk to."

"Yes."

"Do you know anything else about him?"

Slania shook her head. "Not yet, I'm only just getting started."

Hawk went and sat on the sofa and was soon asleep.

When he awoke, he had Slania waving a cup of coffee under his nose. He stretched and said, "I might have to marry you."

"I might have something to say about that," Ilse said. She was sitting at the table, going over what Slania had found.

Hawk looked at his watch. It was five-thirty. "What are you doing up so early?"

"I woke up and you weren't in bed."

Hawk nodded. "Yeah, I was out here hitting on Slania, but she gave me the cold shoulder."

"In your dreams, Romeo."

"Anything new?" he asked.

"Bits and pieces. It turns out that there have been whispers about the Silver Fox around for a while but nothing regarding his identity or location."

"Hey, look at this," Ilse said.

They gathered around her and stared at the screen.

"See this. There is a mention of a White Dove."

"Just the once?" Slania asked.

"No. It has been mentioned several times. Cuthbert

has mentioned meetings with a White Dove and some of the European intelligence agencies have mentioned the name too."

"Maybe Marcel Blanc will know something," Hawk said.

Ilse nodded. "I'll wake Anja. We need to find out."

Ten minutes later, Anja was listening intently to what she was being told. Once finished, she nodded. "I will get us a clearance to go to Paris and activate the mission. I'm sure Mary Thurston will tick it off. Ilse, warn our pilots we need to be up inside two hours."

"Yes, ma'am."

"Jake, get Marcus up. Then make a list of what you need."

"Ma'am."

"It looks like our break is over."

Paris, France

On the outskirts of the city, an abandoned processing factory became their makeshift headquarters. The team huddled around a weathered table, poring over crucial intelligence. While Hawk and Gray prepared to embark on their mission, Anja said, "Slania, take it away."

"Marcel Blanc. He is an advertising exec and all round regular bad guy. An intermediary who sets people up with whatever they need. I've managed to find out that he is dining tonight with this man."

The screen changed, and another man appeared. He looked to be Middle Eastern. "Fuck," Hawk muttered.

"You know him?" Anja asked.

"Fajir Midani. The man is a fucking butcher. He's from Syria."

"Correct," Slania said.

"Why is he meeting with Blanc?" Hawk asked.

"Intel has it that he is in Paris looking for another wife," Slania said. "That would be number four."

"Can I top him, boss?" Hawk asked.

"No. The target is Blanc."

"Roger that."

Slania said, "Be aware, Jake, Midani travels with his own personal entourage of bodyguards. If you get made, expect them to throw everything at you."

"Where is this meeting taking place?"

"A restaurant called Nourriture de Luxe. You will observe and then once Blanc is alone again and leaves, you will pick him up."

"Roger that."

"What are we driving?" Gray asked.

"A Ford Transit."

Hawk made a noise.

Anja looked at him. "Did you say something, Jake?"

"Not a word, boss."

"I didn't think so. Get ready. Gear up."

———

AS NIGHT ENVELOPED THE CITY, its coolness permeated the air. Orange lights suffused their warm glow over the darkened streets, creating an eerie ambiance. Vehicle headlamps sliced through the obscurity, their monotonous rhythm punctuating the silence. All the while, Hawk and Gray waited impatiently, anticipating the arrival of their target.

"Alpha Two, how much bloody longer are we waiting for this prick?" Hawk asked. "We're an hour over as it is."

"Stand by, Bravo One," Ilse replied. Hawk imagined her talking to Anja, asking for orders. Then, a few moments later, "One, Alpha says give it another ten minutes then we'll call it a night."

"Roger that."

After an additional five minutes, a dark green SUV pulled up outside the restaurant. As they watched, Blanc climbed out, flanked by two tall men. They had to be bodyguards.

"Alpha Two, the eagle has landed."

"Roger. Target on site."

Blanc entered the restaurant and disappeared. But only from the outside. Ilse said, "Bravo One, we have eyes on the target."

"Copy, Alpha Two."

Hawk looked out the window at the street. "If he's here, then Midani can't be too far away."

"Yeah," Gray agreed.

"Did you get over that little issue?" Hawk asked him.

"Yeah."

"Good lad."

He was about to say more when there was a knock on the window beside him. Startled, Hawk turned his head while reaching for his P320. The face on the other side of the glass was smiling at him. "Ah fuck. Alpha standby. We could have a bloody problem."

"What do you mean, Jake?"

He ignored the question and signaled toward the side door. "Keep an eye out, Marcus."

"Copy that."

Hawk climbed into the back and opened the door from the inside. Instead of one man there were two. The pair climbed in and sat down. The man who'd been looking through the window, said, "Hello, Jake."

"Hello, Linus," Hawk said. "What are you doing here?"

Linus Rawlins smiled mirthlessly. He indicated to the

other man and said, "Me and Garth are finding out if a twat like you is here to fuck up an MI6 operation."

"I have my own mission," Hawk replied.

"No, you don't. Fuck off."

Hawk felt his anger build but kept it in check. "Who are you after?"

"Fajir Midani. We've got eyes on him and don't need you tipping our hand."

"That's fine, Linus, I'm here for Marcel Blanc. So you can have Midani. Besides, we're not moving on him until he leaves."

Linus shook his head. "We can't have that, Jake. If you take Blanc, and Midani gets wind of it, and spooked, we could lose him."

"So, you're not actually here for Midani, you're just watching him. Is that right?"

"That's right."

"Alpha, did you get that?"

"Roger, Jake."

Hawk's stare hardened. "Can I shoot the bastard in the head to save issues later on?"

"No, put him on."

Hawk took out his earwig and gave it to Linus. "She wants to talk to you."

Frowning, the MI6 man took it and put it in his ear. "Hello?"

"This is Anja Meyer, commander of Task Force Talon, who am I speaking to?"

"Linus Rawlins, ma'am."

"Good. Now the niceties are out of the way, Mr. Rawlins, listen the fuck up."

Rawlins listened for a few minutes before handing the earwig back, then he looked at Garth. "Come on, we're leaving."

Duly chastised, the pair climbed out, and Hawk went back to the front. "Thanks, boss."

"Don't thank me, Jake. This is a one-shot deal. And for crying out loud, don't blow their operation sky high."

"Ma'am."

A few minutes later, Midani showed up with his entourage, and things went to shit.

————

HAWK'S first indication of trouble was the emanation of gunfire from within the restaurant. Midani had gone in with two of his bodyguards while the others had remained outside in their vehicles on the street.

The group was seated at a table out of view of the internal cameras. Obviously, Blanc had used the restaurant before and knew the locations of possible surveillance points. Ilse had mentioned to Hawk that she was blind, to which he had countered with whether they wanted him and Marcus to insert themselves inside.

Anja had come back with a firm *no,* and not long after that, the shots sounded.

"Shots fired! Shots fired!"

"Shots fired from in the restaurant."

The words were garbled as they smashed into each other. Hawk and Marcus grabbed their P320s and scrambled from the van.

More shots sounded, and civilians began spilling from inside, scrambling in every direction in their haste to escape certain death.

"Jake, hold your position," Ilse snapped.

"Be fucked, someone is shooting people in there."

"Just until we get a clearer picture."

"No."

"You'll follow orders, Jake," Anja growled. "Now, do it."

"Fuck!" he exclaimed and stopped in the middle of the street, Gray beside him. Hawk's frustration boiled inside of him.

However, the decision was about to be taken out of his hands. Across the street, the remaining bodyguards of Midani climbed from their SUVs, each of the four armed with automatic weapons.

One of the four opened fire on the crowd dispersing from the restaurant. He was carrying what looked to be a Heckler and Koch MP7. Innocent people started to fall in the doorway and on the sidewalk.

"Shit, sorry, boss," Hawk growled and opened fire.

The shooter fell with a bullet in his head and upper back. One of his comrades whirled and saw Hawk in the middle of the street with his weapon raised. But Gray had seen him move and taken him down before he could respond.

The other two men had already disappeared inside the restaurant.

Hawk said, "Alpha, we're going inside."

He and Gray ran across the street and were greeted by the sound of more shots. Mostly automatic weapons, but Hawk could hear the distinct crack of a handgun. "Alpha Two, what can you see?"

"It looks like they're shooting at a lone figure in a booth toward the rear of the restaurant, Bravo. It's a man and he appears to be wounded."

"Any sign of our target?"

"Negative, Bravo."

Hawk pushed his way inside and stopped abruptly as he looked to assess the situation. Gray stood beside him. Toward the rear of the restaurant, shooters formed a wall as they fired at the location of their wounded target.

Hawk ground his teeth together. "Put them down, Marcus."

They opened fire, not giving the shooters a chance. Within moments, totally oblivious to the threat from behind, each member of the wall was down. The two Talon operators hurried forward through the chaos the shooters had created.

When they reached the cubicle, Hawk swore. "Damn it, Linus, what the fuck have you done?"

"G—Garth. Where is he?"

Hawk looked around and saw the other MI6 man down and dead, blood-soaked and unmoving. "Sorry, Linus, he's fucked."

A lot like you, Hawk thought, looking at the three bullet wounds in him.

Rawlins gave him a wry grin. "I thought y—you would screw it u—up."

"So you came in here to make sure I wouldn't."

"Fucked it my—myself."

"Bravo, I have your target getting into an SUV out the rear of the restaurant," Ilse said. "You need to move."

"Roger, Alpha Two." He looked at Rawlins. "Sorry, mate, I have to go."

Rawlins nodded. "Be seeing you, Jake."

"You too, Linus. Marcus, we have to roll now."

As they ran toward the door, Gray said, "Your mate must have got Midani. At least he went out in style."

They ran across the street, wet after a brief shower during their time inside. Scrambling into their respective seats in the front of the Transit van, Hawk started the motor, turned on the wipers to clear the windshield, then put it in gear and pulled away from the sidewalk. "Alpha Three, I need a course for intercept."

"Wait One, Bravo. Keep going that direction."

Hawk pressed the gas pedal to the floor, the vehicle

powering forward like a beast unleashed on the damp street as a surge of adrenaline hit his circulatory system.

"Jake, turn left up ahead, then right."

"Copy." Hawk's response was steady, focused.

As they approached the turn, Hawk braked hard, the tires protesting on the wet asphalt. The van's rear fish-tailed, threatening to spin out of control. The orange glow of streetlamps painted streaks on the wet windshield, creating a disorienting dance of light.

Another hard turn, and Hawk felt the vehicle's weight shift. Up ahead, a vehicle bounced as it crossed a side street. Hawk's instincts kicked in as he blew through the same intersection.

Behind them, the screech of tires could be heard as a Peugeot spun wildly after the driver slammed on the brakes to avoid a collision.

"You trying to kill me, Jake?" Gray asked.

"Not tonight, old chap, I don't have time to dig a hole."

"Alpha Three, where is he going?" Gray asked.

"No idea, Bravo Two."

"Oh crap," Hawk growled.

Gray was on the verge of asking Hawk what was amiss, but was then able to see for himself. Rain, thick and relentless, started pelting the windshield like a barrage of bullets. The wipers going full speed couldn't keep up with the great dollops of water that blurred the city lights, creating a surreal dance of orange and yellow.

Through the increasing downpour, Hawk spotted their quarry, a sleek black sedan turning left up ahead. His adrenaline surged, as they were closing in. But as Hawk eased off the gas pedal for the turn, he misjudged the braking distance. Panic flickered across his face, too late to correct his error.

The van skidded, tires losing grip on the wet asphalt. Gray's knuckles whitened as he gripped the door handle.

The world spun, wild, disorienting. The intersection loomed, and Hawk pumped the brakes harder. The vehicle twisted out of control and leaped onto the sidewalk.

The black sedan vanished around another corner, mocking them. "Damn it," Hawk growled angrily. "Why couldn't you get us a real vehicle? We can't lose them now."

Once again, Hawk floored the pedal, and the chase continued. The rain fell even harder, and as Hawk made the turn further along the street, he knew they were done. Ahead of them lay a laneway of emptiness, not even any tire marks on the saturated road. It was a street of nothing but dark shadows.

"Alpha One, copy?" Hawk said almost despondently.

"Alpha One copies."

"We've lost him, boss. Unless Three can still see him, we're done."

"That's a negative, Bravo. He's gone. Come home."

"Roger that. Fuck."

CHAPTER FIVE

Paris, France

"WHAT HAPPENED?" Anja asked Hawk when they got back to the factory.

"MI6 screwed their op trying to make sure we wouldn't," Hawk replied. "The only good piece of news was that Midani is fucked. Oh, and the Transit van didn't help the situation."

"Now it's time to reset," Anja said, ignoring the jibe.

Hawk turned to Ilse. "Is there anything that indicates where he went?"

"Nothing. We're back at square one."

"In the morning, while you are trying to find Blanc, there might be someone I can see who may have heard about the Chasseurs."

"Who?" Anja asked.

"An old SAS buddy. He worked a lot of personal security in France and other places. He might have heard something."

"Okay, you and Marcus go and do that. In the meantime, everyone turn in."

THE FACTORY WAS COLD, but at least it was dry. Hawk had set up next to Ilse, and they lay there in the darkness, listening to the creaks and groans of the factory's framework. Finally, Hawk said, "It sounds like this thing wants to fall on our bloody heads."

"Do you think your friend will know something, Jake?" Ilse asked.

"I don't know, love, but it can't hurt to ask." He paused. "What was the fallout from MI6?"

"Nothing, really. I mean, what could they say? Their own people screwed it up."

"Yeah."

There was a long silence before Ilse said, "Night, Jake."

"Night."

"Love you."

"Love you too."

———

JOHNNY MACK SAT in his black BMW across the street from a swanky café, eating a salad sandwich while waiting for the banking executive to emerge from her breakfast with her *bit on the side*.

Taking another bite, he felt a piece of lettuce hit his shirt. "Ah, fuck," he growled and picked it off and stuffed it into his mouth. He'd been working this job for two months now, and all he ever seemed to do was sit in a vehicle while the woman met her boyfriend or screwed his brains out in a hotel room.

But what the hell, it paid okay.

There was a tap at the driver's window. Mack turned and saw a familiar face grinning back at him. "Fuck me."

Hawk walked around the front of the BMW and climbed in the passenger seat. "Johnny Fucking Mack, how are you, mate?"

"Shit, Jake, what do you want?"

"Just dropped by to see an old mate."

Mack rolled his eyes. "Like I said, what do you want?"

"I need some information. Me and my team are working on something you might be able to help with?"

"Team? What team?" Mack asked.

"Me and a few others, we're taking some bad people off the board of life."

"Oh, yeah?" There was skepticism in his voice.

"Ever heard of the Chasseurs?" Hawk asked.

"I might have."

"Great. I told the boss you'd be able to help."

"I didn't say I could help you, Jake. Just that I might have heard about them."

"So? Who are they?"

"Mercenaries. They specialize in kidnap for hire. Former French Foreign Legion."

"French?"

"Yes."

"Who runs them?"

"No idea," Mack said.

"You sure? Anything would help."

"Sorry, mate, that's about it."

"Okay, thanks," Hawk said.

"I didn't help much," Mack said.

"More than what we had."

"Are you going after them?"

"Yeah."

"Keep your head down," Mack said.

Hawk climbed out of the BMW just as a blue van pulled up across the street. Curiously, he watched as a woman alighted. She had long silver-blonde hair, virtually platinum. She wore dark sunglasses and an ankle-length coat. Hawk frowned. It wasn't that bloody cold. Realization dawned as to her identity. "You cheeky bitch."

Suddenly, the van's side door slid open, and five men tumbled out, all armed with AK-19s. Then, the woman flipped her coat back and revealed her own weapon.

Hawk dived behind the BMW, putting the engine block between himself and the shooters. The roar as the weapons opened fire was deafening. The passenger door flew open, and Mack slithered out. "What the fuck did you do, Jake?"

"Maybe I didn't call her back," Hawk called out as he pulled his P320.

Mack pulled a Glock and said, "Only you could bring shit down like this. Good to see nothing has fucking changed."

"It's a habit," Hawk threw back at him.

"Yeah, a fucking bad one."

As the deadly storm came their way, Hawk reached for his cell. While it rang, he fired a couple of shots at the shooters. Beside him, Mack had his own weapon, loosing shots in retaliation. Hawk saw it and said, "What the fuck is that?"

"You know what it is, Jake. It's a P30."

"My dick is bigger than that, Mack. When are you going to get a man's gun?"

"Just shut up and fucking shoot."

Hawk put the cell to his ear. "Jake? Is that you? What's going on?"

"Hi, love," he said to Ilse. "You know that White Dove bird you mentioned?"

"What about her, Jake? Is that gunfire?"

Hawk rose up and fired another couple of rounds. "Yeah. I think I've found her. What do you want me to do with her?"

"Damn it, Jake, why you?"

"I guess I'm just lucky," he replied. "Just thought I'd let you know what was happening. Talk later."

The call disconnected, and Mack stared at him. "Are you bloody serious?"

"All part of having a loved one in your life, Mack."

"Dickhead."

"Just shut up and shoot the bitch with the blonde hair," Hawk shouted as a storm of bullets hammered into the BMW.

"Who is she?" Mack asked as he started firing.

"Some silly cow called the *White Dove*."

Mack dropped down like a brick had been dropped on his head. "Shit, Jake."

"What now?" Hawk demanded, firing at a concealed shooter.

"You don't know?"

"No fucking idea, mate."

"She's like the queen of the European underworld. She has killers at her fingertips and commands a network of despair."

Hawk forgot about shooting for a moment and stared at his friend. "You're taking the piss, aren't you?"

"I wish I was, mate."

Hawk rose up and opened fire again with a loud snarl. He blew off the rest of the magazine in his P320 as words tumbled from his mouth. "Of all the fucking situations a man finds himself in, this one takes the bloody cake. In a bleedin' gunfight with Europe's second most deadly female."

"Who's the most?" Mack asked as he reloaded.

"My boss. Former German intelligence."

"Enough bloody said. What are we going to do?"

Hawk looked over the hood of the destroyed BMW. He counted at least eight shooters plus the woman. He dropped back down and said, "You ever heard of the marvelous British invention called a strategic withdrawal?"

"Roger that."

"Then start bloody running, mate."

Both men came to their feet, and with heads down, ran for their lives.

———

ACROSS THE STREET, the woman known as the White Dove reloaded her CZ Scorpion Evo 3 submachine gun. Beside her, Vadim said, "They are running away."

The woman emptied the magazine after them in a long burst of anger. "Shit. Let them go. We will find them again. Or they us."

Vadim began barking orders at his men who fell back to the van. All around them on the street was carnage. Wounded and dead. Collateral damage from the way the White Dove's killers indiscriminately fired their weapons.

Once they were all back in the van, Vadim engaged it into gear, and they drove away. The mission had been a failure. She wasn't used to that. It burned deep.

———

GRAY PICKED them up several streets away while they were on the run. They dropped Mack at the station where he could get a train to England. He was advised to keep a low profile there until it all blew over. Meanwhile, Hawk and Gray returned to the team's base of operations.

"Talk to me, Jake," Anja said as soon as he entered the factory.

"She's a nasty cow, that White Dove bird," he

growled. "She pulled up with her team and just opened up on us."

"No doubt about the target?" Ilse asked.

Hawk shook his head. "None whatsoever. I was it."

"Description?" Anja asked.

"Six-foot, silver-blonde hair, almost white. Sunglasses, pale face, built like an athlete, though it was hard to tell with the coat she was wearing. Was using a bloody Scorpion. Definitely, weapons trained."

"Slania is trying to get footage of her."

"Mack called her the queen of the underworld. Says she has killers at her fingertips."

Anja nodded. "Did you take any hits?"

"No."

"Okay, take some time while we work out what to do next."

"Yes, boss."

Ilse followed him over to a coffee machine. She touched his arm. "Are you okay, Jake?"

"Yeah. I'm fine. But I tell you what, girl, this White Dove cow, she is bloody dangerous."

"Then we better find her."

"What about Marcel Blanc?"

"We're still working on that. For all we know, he could be out of the city by now."

"If he has any sense, he will be."

Ilse nodded. "Get some rest."

———

ILSE'S CELL BUZZED, and she picked it up before it could go to the message bank. "Yes?"

"Ilse? Karl Hoffman, I got your message."

Hoffman was an intelligence officer in the German

Federal Intelligence Service. "Hello, Karl, thank you for returning my call."

"Anything for an old friend. What can I do for you?"

"What do you know about a woman called the White Dove?"

On the other end of the call, Hoffman let out a long breath. Ilse knew from his reaction it wasn't going to be good. "Came onto the scene about two years ago. First off, the name was associated with arms trafficking. Then, it was stepped up a notch when a shipment of French girls was intercepted passing through Germany. Intel had them bought by the White Dove and they were being shipped to Russia."

"For any specific reason?" Ilse asked.

"Prostitution, high-class escorts, to be sold to the rich. Take your pick."

"So, she is a buyer and seller? Is that it?" Ilse asked.

"She would be what you call a high-end trafficker. Has her own team run by a Russian called Vadim."

"Do you have a name for her?"

"Sorry, Ilse," Hoffman replied. "That is the million-dollar question. What we do know is that she is dangerous. I know of three intelligence agencies who have sent people after her and none of them have been seen since. We were one of them. How are you mixed up with her?"

"We're going to take her out of an equation that we're working on," Ilse replied.

"I wish you luck, Ilse, I really do."

"Before you go, Karl, I have another for you."

"I'm listening."

"The Silver Fox."

"Russian Oligarch, no name, no home address. A ghost."

"Man, I wish I had stayed in bed this morning."

"By the sounds of it, you should have. Is there anything else?"

"No. Thanks, Karl."

"I'd say stay safe, Ilse, but in this case, I think I'm better off saying stay alive."

"You are so kind."

With the call done, Ilse went to find Slania. Anja was standing there with her, so it worked out that she didn't have to tell what she had learned twice. Once she was done, Anja said, "So, we're hunting ghosts again."

"Maybe not," Ilse said. "The White Dove is a buyer. That means she is in Paris to make a purchase. She has to be. If we can find Blanc, then just maybe we can find her."

Anja nodded. "Okay, let's double our efforts. See what we can come up with. Good work, Ilse."

"Ma'am."

Later that afternoon, Slania uncovered their first breadcrumb. "Ilse, I might have something."

Ilse went over to where Slania was working and looked over her shoulder, looking at a photo on her screen. It showed a man in a hotel foyer. "Who is he?"

"Amir Al-Mahmoud from Saudi Arabia. He has a harem of wives back in his country any man would be proud of. There are also known links to terror organizations. He doesn't leave his country much. When he does, it is usually for something important."

"Why have you flagged him?"

"He could be here to buy another wife," Slania said. She changed the picture, and Amir was talking to another man. "That is Julien Moreau. Interpol has him linked to underground auctions that sell anything from weapons to people."

"Nice piece of work."

"Yes, ma'am."

"Tell me what you're thinking, Slania."

"We shift our focus from Blanc to Moreau."

Ilse nodded. "Do it. I'm guessing that we have twenty-four hours to come up with something."

"Leave it with me."

———

A KNOCK on the hotel suite door drew the attention of the White Dove from her laptop. She glanced at Vadim who was reaching for his sidearm. Following suit, she watched her bodyguard walk toward the door. When he reached it, he said, "Who is it?"

"Julien Moreau."

Vadim glanced at his boss, and she nodded. He opened the door, and the Frenchman entered. Relaxing, the White Dove let go of her weapon but left it on the table where she was working.

Moreau smiled at her. "Svetlana, it is good to see you."

Svetlana Orlova leaned back in her seat and said, "It has been a while, Julien."

"Too long," he replied with a broad grin. He reached inside his suit jacket and withdrew an envelope, placing it on the table. "I have your official invitation for tomorrow night's masquerade party. I trust you are still joining us."

Svetlana picked up the envelope and fingered the stark white paper with gold embossing. "I trust there will be a good variety of product?"

"The best in a while," Moreau replied. "Are you in the market for anything in particular?"

"I think something will take my fancy."

"I'm sure it will. I have heard Declan will be there, too."

"How interesting. Is there a reason?"

"Let's just say he has a larger percentage than usual in

this market," Moreau replied. "I'm sure he will be pleased to see you."

Svetlana looked at the salacious smile on Moreau's face. "Get your mind out of the gutter, Julien."

The smile disappeared. "Yes, sorry."

"Besides, who I sleep with is no concern of yours. Is there anything else?"

"No, I think that is it."

"Good. Join me for a drink."

CHAPTER SIX

Paris, France

IT WAS JUST before noon the following day that Slania managed to pick up Moreau. He was found on security feed from a café in the city not far from the Eifel Tower. "Now I've found him, he should be easy to track."

Anja nodded. "Jake, Marcus, time to go to work."

Hawk and Gray left in a dark SUV. They drove as fast as they could into the city, and as they approached the café vicinity, Hawk said, "Alpha, comms check."

"Copy, Bravo," Ilse replied. "Target is walking along Avenue de Suffren. There is a jeweler up ahead on your right. He is there but still in motion."

"Copy, Alpha. I can see him. Pull over, Marcus."

Gray pulled the SUV over, and Hawk said, "Alpha, One and Two are proceeding on foot."

"Roger that."

"What are we going to do, Jake?" Gray asked as he stepped onto the sidewalk.

"Play it by ear, old mate."

The operators started following Moreau at a reasonable distance. Meanwhile, Slania was tracking him using cameras.

Up ahead, there was another café with a red awning out front. Hawk and Marcus watched as Moreau disappeared inside. "Feel like a coffee, Mucker?"

"Don't mind if I do."

Entering the café, the pair found a table far enough away to not be suspicious. Over the comms, Slania said, "Get close enough so I can link to his cell. Maybe we might find something on it."

As they sat down, a waitress approached them and asked in French, "What would you like?"

"Two coffees, please love," Hawk replied. "White, one sugar."

Gray leaned over after the waitress had gone and said, "What the fuck is wrong with you? We only drink black and none."

"Screams military old mate."

"He wouldn't know that."

"Can't take that chance," Hawk replied.

"Bravo One, I've managed to get into his cell. Nothing out of the ordinary—oh shit."

"That sounds good," Hawk said quietly.

"I have Marcel Blanc outside the café on his way in."

The next voice Hawk heard was Ilse's. "One, you need to get out. There is a possibility he knows your face."

Hawk looked up at the doorway and saw Blanc already entering. "Too late."

Hawk moved his chair swiftly so that his back was to the doorway. Gray was now positioned to look over his shoulder. Ilse said, "What are you doing, One?"

"Working with what we have, Alpha."

"I hope you know what you are doing, Bravo One."

This time, it was Anja. "This is the strongest lead we've had."

"Head's up," Gray said. "Moreau is handing an envelope over to Blanc."

"I have it," Slania said.

Blanc took the envelope and put it into his jacket pocket. Then he stood up and started to leave. "Boss, what do you want us to do?" Gray asked.

Anja didn't hesitate. "Go with Blanc. We'll leave Moreau in play. Blanc is the target."

As they got to their feet, Gray said, "Roger that."

Hawk and Gray followed him out of the café and onto the street. They turned left and kept at a distance to not alert him. It didn't last long. Slania said, "Bravo, I think your friend at the café made you. I don't know how. He just reached for his cell."

"And I know who he just called," Hawk replied, watching Blanc grab his phone.

After a few moments, Blanc turned and looked directly at Hawk and Gray.

Marcus said, "He's made us, Jake."

"Pick a number between one and ten," Hawk replied.

"Why?"

"Do it."

"Three."

Hawk nodded. "Good choice. Now start running."

"What—oh fuck!"

Gray started running after the fleeing man. Hawk called after him, "Don't let him get away."

Up ahead, Blanc disappeared around the corner of a building into an alleyway. Gray swung around the corner and watched Blanc vanish behind a garbage truck coming toward him.

The former para moved over to the left wall, not slowing, even though the gap narrowed when the truck passed.

The gap was closing. Blanc wasn't much of a runner. Gray picked up his pace just as Blanc disappeared out the far end of the alley.

When Gray emerged, he almost hit a pedestrian. The man swore at him in French for being careless. The former para ignored him.

Blanc had cut off the sidewalk near a tall streetlamp. He ducked out onto the tarmac and stopped suddenly as a vehicle almost ran him down. There was a small screech of tires as the car stopped.

Blanc made to go around it, but Gray was on top of him. Gray hit him from behind, and both men spilled across the hood. The impact with the street jarred through Gray's body. He let out a yelp of pain before staggering to his feet.

A fist crashed against his jaw, and he tasted blood inside his mouth. He staggered back, and Blanc followed him. The Frenchman swung again. Gray blocked the blow before it could connect. Then he parried with a straight left and then an arching right.

The Frenchman staggered back. Gray followed him this time and hit him twice more. Blanc staggered back into the path of traffic, and just like you see in the movies, he was hammered down by a bus.

"For crying out fucking loud, mate, what was that?" Hawk demanded, looking at the crushed body of the Frenchman.

"Thanks for your fucking help, *mate*."

"We needed him alive, not bloody spread all over the street like raspberry jam. The boss is going to freak. You're fucked, mate."

"Why me? You're in charge."

Hawk looked around at the crowd that was gathering. "Come on, before one of these scousers realizes that this is a great bloody photo opportunity."

They started to turn away when Gray noticed the envelope on the ground. He bent down and picked it up. "Must have fallen out of his pocket."

"Worry about it later."

As they began retracing their steps, Anja was in their ears, trying to find out what was happening. Finally, she had had enough. "One of you bastards better talk to me or I'll fucking shoot you myself."

"Got you, Alpha," Gray said. "We must have been in a dead spot."

Hawk rolled his eyes.

"Speaking of dead, is Bravo One there with you?" A pause. "And before you lie, we have you on security feed."

"Ah—I'm here, boss," Hawk said.

"Good. Now were we seeing things, or did our target just get hit by a bloody bus?"

"He's had better days."

"Fuck." There was a muffled sound before they heard Anja say, "You talk to them, I've had enough of their shit."

Ilse took over, saying, "One, Two, return to base for debrief."

The comms went silent, and Hawk glared at Gray. "See what you fucking did?"

"Whatever."

———

"SOMEONE TELL me why our main lead is being scraped up off the street and police are crawling all over the scene? Not to mention the calls I've had to make," Anja demanded of her two field operatives.

Hawk looked at Gray and winked. "Best of luck, mate."

Gray said, "I was chasing him, and he ended up in front of a bus after he resisted being apprehended."

"That's it?" There was sarcasm in Anja's voice.

The former para reached into his jacket pocket. "I did manage to get this while we were having our barney."

Hawk stared at Gray. This was his way of getting back at him for chasing Blanc. Gray passed the envelope over to Ilse who opened it. She looked it over and said, "It is an invitation to a masquerade party."

"Where?" asked Anja, her mind already working.

"A place called La Vue."

Slania started working. A few moments later, she said, "East Paris. It is an old building that was renovated a few years back. It is owned by a Belgian company."

"Interesting. What is the name on it? For the invitation?"

"There is no name," Slania said. "Just a number."

"That could work in our favor," Anja said. "When is it?"

"It looks like tonight," Ilse replied.

"Good. Slania, Ilse, dust off your ball gowns, you're going to a masquerade party."

"Why not us?" Hawk asked.

"Because by now, they know you, Jake," Ilse said. "Less chance of me and Slania being recognized."

"Shall we go as a couple?" Slania asked.

Ilse grinned. "I think so."

"Fine, go and glam up." Anja turned to Hawk and Gray. "You two will be geared up and close by as a QRF. Don't mess it up."

———————

ILSE AND SLANIA looked glamorous in long, form-hugging dresses. Slania's was black, plunging at the back, showing just enough cleavage at the front and a lot of tattoos. Ilse was wearing a backless red number, revealing a lot of flesh, including the angel tattoo on her shoulder blade. She called it her good luck charm. Both dresses were designed so that the lower skirt could be torn away, if required, to enable them to engage in hand-to-hand combat.

Both were armed, but not with handguns. Ilse had a stiletto-type knife on the inside of her right thigh. Slania, had her knife in a pouch hooked to her necklace, which was secreted under her hair at the back. Both also wore earwigs for constant communication. Last, there were small cameras in the pendants on their necklaces.

The downside of their outfits meant they were unable to be protected by a Synoprathetic suit. They each dropped their glittery white mask, effectively covering their face.

"How do we look?" Ilse asked.

"Very lovely," Hawk replied. "You'll be turning heads left and right."

"This is a first for me," she said. "I've never gone undercover as a lesbian before."

Slania winked at her. "Don't worry, babe, I've got you covered."

Hawk parked their van two doors down from the building known as La Vue, and the girls slipped out through the side door, and started along the sidewalk.

Ilse said, "Can you all hear me?"

"Comms check would have sufficed," Hawk replied.

"Shut up," Slania said.

"Yes, comms are good," Hawk reported. "Boss, how about you?"

"Comms are good, and the cameras are working," Anja confirmed.

"Roger that. Let's do this."

Joining the queue for entry, they were surprised at how steadily it was moving, and within minutes had reached the rope bollards. Two large security guards blocking their passage were checking tickets.

"Both penguin suits are armed," Ilse said quietly.

The bigger of the two leered at them and said, "Do you have a ticket?"

"I think I have it here somewhere," Ilse responded in fluent French as she dug through her purse.

She withdrew the letter and passed it over. The man looked at it, handed it back, and said, "Take the stairs down on the right."

Stepping through the doorway, they glanced around, taking their time to give their boss a good look at the interior. A further two guards, both armed, stood at the top of the descending stairway. It would seem that an equal number of party guests were going up as well as down.

"Invitation, please?" the guard on the right asked.

Once again it was produced, then scrutinized before being handed back. This time, the guard said into a hidden mic, "Fifty-four, party of two."

Slania glanced at Ilse who remained stoic behind her mask. They both waited before the guard said, "Proceed. Have a nice evening."

They walked steadily down the stairs, their high heels clicking on each step as they went. Once at the bottom, they were greeted by a waiter holding a tray of filled champagne flutes. Ilse selected two, passed one to Slania and smiled. "Shall we?"

Slania slipped her hand into Ilse's, and they started through the crowd of party-goers. Men wearing suits or tuxedoes, the women in dresses or gowns, all wearing masks.

"Looks impressive," Slania said.

"Very."

"Cameras are useless in this bloody environment," Anja growled.

Every now and then, as the pair walked past someone, they would bow their heads in acknowledgment. Be they man or woman.

The room was huge, the floor above supported by granite pillars. The floor was laid with large slabs of travertine. A woman with almost as many tats as Slania walked past. "See anyone you know?" Ilse asked cheekily.

"Maybe. I'd need to get her clothes off to find out for certain."

"So, tats are your thing?"

"Oh, hell yeah. If I see a good tat on a man or woman, I've already got them undressed."

"Maybe I should have worn a full dress."

"Too late now."

"Anything on the phone yet, boss?" Ilse asked.

"Still trying to hook in. Just keep mingling."

A tall woman in a blue dress walked past Ilse, her hand extending to touch her arm. It lingered there longer than social norms dictated, and their eyes made contact before she kept going. Slania leaned close and said, "Someone was flirting."

For the next hour, they walked around fighting a losing battle. Ilse said, "We need something, boss, or we need to get gone."

"I'm trying," Anja replied.

"Wait, go back," Hawk said.

"What do you mean?"

"Slania, swing back to your left."

Slania frowned but turned anyway. The figure came into view on Hawk's end. "There, stop there."

"What are we looking at?" she asked.

"The blonde in front of you."

The two women caught her straight away. "Got her. Purple dress, black mask."

"That's her," Hawk said. "That is the cow who shot at me with all her friends."

"Are you saying she's the White Dove, Jake?" Ilse asked.

"I'd bet my bollocks on it."

"You need to be really positive, Jake," Anja said.

"It's her, boss."

"All right, stay on her."

Suddenly, the lighting changed, and a circle started to form in the center of the room. All of the party-goers moved outward. The room darkened, and a spotlight lit the area where a man walked to. He wore a suit and top hat like an old-time ringmaster.

"This ought to be interesting," Ilse said in a low voice. "Use this as an opportunity to get close to the target."

Ilse and Slania adjusted their position to get closer to Svetlana. Anja said, "You are good there."

It was now that the ringmaster started his monologue. "Ladies and gentlemen, welcome to what one would call the most intriguing part of the evening. I hope you brought your payment devices with you because you will need them."

A round of polite applause was followed by a murmur of anticipation.

"He's English," Ilse said.

"I'll see if I can get an ID on this man," Anja said.

The ringmaster continued. "On offer tonight, we have five lots. From deepest darkest Africa to the steaming jungles of Myanmar. There will be something here for everyone...provided you have the money."

He let out a laugh.

"Without further ado, let's get *started!*"

He stepped to one side as the floor opened up, and moments later, a platform rose from below.

"But first, ladies and gentlemen, let's start with a

beauty from Switzerland. Her father is a banker, and her mother a beauty queen."

The girl appeared inside a glass cage. She was dressed in a gold bikini, so as much flesh as possible was exposed. She looked drugged.

"How the fuck do they get away with this shit?" Slania whispered into Ilse's ear.

The ringmaster said, "Let's open the bidding at two hundred and fifty thousand dollars."

Within a few heartbeats, the bidding was up to $450,000. Not long after that, she was sold. The ringmaster let out a yelp of joy, "I'm sure you will be truly happy with your purchase, sir."

"What do we do, Anja?" Ilse asked.

"Remain on task, Ilse. I'm gathering intel as we speak."

"Next!" the ringmaster exclaimed.

The floor gave way, and several minutes later. "Lot two, ladies and gentlemen, is a beautiful specimen from the slopes of Mount Fuji."

The young woman, as announced, was Japanese. She, too, wore the gold bikini, and her alabaster skin stood out like a snow-covered landscape. "This young lady has lineage which can be traced back to the emperor himself. She may be tiny, but she is a fine-looking young woman. Where are we going to start? Three hundred?"

A hand flew up, and as like the first, the price climbed rapidly until the young woman was sold for just under half a million.

With that done, the ringmaster stepped back into the action. "Now, ladies and gentlemen, we have something more exotic for you all. Lot three comes all the way from Africa."

The floor came back up and contained within the glass cage were three women and a man. All were a deep mahogany color and rippled with muscle.

"Now, ladies and gentlemen, as you can see, this is indeed a special lot. They speak for themselves so there will be no more from me. Someone, open the bidding."

"One million," came a voice from the crowd.

"Two million," came another.

"I have an ID for the idiot in the penguin suit," Anja said. "You'll like this. His name is Declan Hunter."

"Hunter as in Chasseur?"

"Yes."

"Oh, wonderful."

"He is the head of Hunter Enterprises here in Paris. It is a multinational business which sells telecommunications devices."

"And we all know what else he does," Hawk said.

"Fifty million."

The words drew attention directly to the woman known as the White Dove. A murmur rippled through the room, punctuated by a few gasps of surprise.

"Fifty million. Is there anyone who would like to better the offer?"

When nothing else was forthcoming, Hunter said, "Then I guess the bidding is closed for this lot. Let's take a brief recess, and then we shall resume for the remainder."

"Okay," Anja said. "Time to leave."

"What about the others?" Ilse asked, meaning the two remaining lots.

"We have all we need."

"But—"

"I will take care of it. I have alerted Interpol."

They turned to leave when Ilse felt a hand on her arm. She turned back and saw the White Dove staring at her through the eye holes of her mask. "Leaving so soon?"

"Yes, we have to go."

"Really?"

"Yes, we have a flight to catch to Antwerp tomorrow," Slania said.

"Surely you could join me for a drink?"

Slania started to speak. "We really—"

"One drink won't hurt," Ilse said, cutting her off.

"What are you doing, Ilse?" Anja asked.

"Good," the woman before them said, pleased. "Follow me."

CHAPTER SEVEN

Paris, France

THEY ENTERED a small room complete with lounge and mini bar along the side wall. On the other wall was a small screen which showed the main room. With the woman came her bodyguard. A big, broad-shouldered man with blond hair and a flattop haircut. He stood in a corner and remained silent.

The woman took off her mask, revealing an attractive face and piercing eyes. Her eyeshadow matched the purple of her lips and dress. "I'm glad to be rid of that. It is so stifling."

Ilse and Slania removed theirs. "What are we doing here?"

The White Dove poured them drinks. "I hope you like vodka."

"As long as it burns," Slania said.

She passed them their drinks. Ilse said, "You didn't answer the question."

Svetlana took a sip of her drink and licked her lips. "Let me say that you intrigued me."

"Wearing a dress and a mask intrigues you?"

"It's what lies beneath. Just the look tells me a lot."

"Oh, how so?"

She indicated Slania. "The black dress, the lipstick, tattoos. That tells me she is the more dominant one in your relationship. You have a red dress, lighter lipstick, no tattoos. That tells me you are more feminine. You like the finer things, whereas your partner is used to taking what she wants."

"Okay."

"So, does she?"

"Does she what?" Ilse asked.

"Take you."

In the van, Hawk almost choked on his coffee. He let a grin come to his lips. "If she only knew," he whispered to himself.

"You might be surprised," Ilse replied to Svetlana.

"Really? I find that hard to believe."

"Believe what you want."

The White Dove looked at her thoughtfully. "Then maybe you should prove it."

"I beg your pardon?"

Svetlana looked at Slania. "I will give you five million in American dollars if you allow me to sleep with your woman."

Slania grinned but remained silent.

"Is this how you get your women?" Ilse asked. "Money?"

"I don't have time to mess around with seduction. I am a busy woman."

"Sorry, I don't think so."

The White Dove gave them a sorrowful look. "I was hoping to have some fun before I killed you both. Oh, well."

"What do you mean, kill us?"

Over the comms, Ilse heard Hawk say, "We're on our way."

Svetlana smiled. "At first, I wasn't sure. But once the masks came off, I knew who you were immediately."

"And just who are we?" Ilse asked, buying more time.

"The mercenaries who stopped and dismantled Medusa. But when you cut the heads off the snake, more shall appear elsewhere."

"Don't I know it," Ilse said.

Sudden gunfire could be heard, and Ilse said, "Bravo, small room, hallway, back left."

Svetlana smiled, showing her teeth. "Very good. Now, let's have some fun."

———

HAWK AND GRAY burst the van at a run. Both men had tactical vests on but were only armed with their P320s. A crowded floor was no place for an assault weapon. Ahead of them, as they approached the entrance, the guard on the door was still putting people through. However, when he saw Hawk and Gray coming with their ski masks on, he moved for his gun.

"Boss, rules of engagement?"

"Treat them as hostile, Bravo One."

"Roger that," Hawk replied and fired his weapon just as the guard got his free.

The bullet punched into the man's head, and he dropped stone dead in front of the entrance. Many of the party-goers began screaming and scattering in different directions. In Hawk's ear, Anja said, "Don't shoot any innocent bystanders. That would make me rather upset."

"Copy."

They were about to breach when gunfire erupted from

the two guards at the top of the stairs. Hawk and Gray took cover on the other side of the doorway. They looked at each other and nodded. Then, just as the fire stopped, they went through. Hawk took the shooter on the left. Two shots. X-ray down. Gray took the one on the right with the same result. They ran for the stairs and began to descend. A shooter appeared at the bottom, looking in their direction. Hawk fired again. This man staggered before Hawk had to shoot him once more to put him down.

By the time they reached the ballroom, it was chaos. The gunfire had caused the crowd to scatter. Now, the boys were fighting a rising tide as well as the armed guards.

ILSE THREW herself at the White Dove. Their bodies crashed together like solid pieces of wood. Ilse threw a right elbow at the woman, and the force of the blow knocked her back.

"Fucking bitch," Ilse snarled and threw a punch that landed solidly, flattening her lips.

The White Dove lurched back, steadied herself, and smiled. There was blood on her teeth. She ripped the bottom of her dress away and exposed a stiletto strapped to her thigh.

She grabbed the handle and pulled it clear, waving it in front of herself. Ilse nodded. "Okay, you want to do it that way."

Ilse mirrored the woman's actions, rending the skirt of her own dress, and exposed her knife. She pulled it clear and said, "Come on, let's party."

They came together and drew back. Ilse felt the burn in her left arm as her opponent's knife sliced a shallow cut in her skin. She hissed in frustration and gathered herself before they clashed once again.

Meanwhile, Slania closed the gap between herself and Vadim. He swung a savage blow which she evaded, and while he was off balance, she withdrew her own knife and plunged it deep into the muscles of his left shoulder.

Vadim lurched back, and the knife was torn free of Slania's grasp. He looked down at the weapon and then shifted his gaze on Slania. He smiled at her.

"Shit, fuck," she growled, realizing she was in trouble.

The big man pulled the knife free and tossed it aside. Slania tore her skirt free and twisted like a ballet dancer, her right foot, coming high and connecting with Vadim's jaw.

He rocked back and closed the gap, swinging a stunning blow. It caught Slania on the shoulder and knocked her sideways. She landed on a small table which collapsed under her weight. She let out a grunt of pain and then a moan. Vadin bent over her and lifted her by the throat.

Across the room, Ilse was still engaged with Svetlana. Both were now bleeding from various cuts, although nothing too serious.

Svetlana lunged for Ilse who dropped and swept a foot to the right. It took the Russian woman's legs from beneath her, and she fell hard. Svetlana's head was in range, and Ilse kicked out.

Svetlana rolled away just as the blow hit.

Vadim slammed Slania against the wall, and the air rushed from her lungs. Refilling them became an issue as the big man was slowly strangling her. She brought her knee up and caught Vadim in the groin. He grunted, and his grip loosened. Bringing her arms up between his, she forced the Russin to release her.

Dropping the short distance to the floor, Slania slumped against the wall. Vadim came close, and she reached out with her right hand and grabbed a good handful of his manhood. He stopped suddenly as she commenced a vicious squeeze. "How do you like that, motherfucker?"

On the other side of the room, Ilse and the White Dove were still trying to find a hole in each other's defenses. Svetlana said, "My father will be pleased when you are gone."

Father? It suddenly fell into place. White Dove, Silver Fox. "Alpha, did you get that?"

"Roger. Bring that bitch in."

Ilse's face hardened. "Right, you fucking cow, time to get serious."

She stepped closer, and the lights went out.

———

SOMEONE CAME at Hawk from the side and crashed into him. They hit the floor, and the Brit finished on top. Placing the P320 against the man's head, he realized he was sitting on an unarmed assailant. "Don't be a fucking hero."

He brought the butt down between the man's eyes and knocked him out. Gray appeared beside him and dragged Hawk to his feet. "No time for cuddles, old man."

"Shut up."

A guard appeared with an MP5. Gray took aim and fired a bullet into his chest. A red blossom sprouted on the guard's white shirt beneath his open jacket. He hit the floor and started to drown in his own blood.

Another guard opened fire at them, spraying wildly. One of the panicked auction goers cried out and fell to the floor. "Marcus, I don't have a shot!" Hawk called out.

"Got him!" Gray opened fire with a clear line of sight.

The two shots struck home and sent the shooter to the floor.

"Keep going," Hawk shouted.

Fleeing men and women from the masquerade party crashed into them. One woman stumbled at Hawk's feet. He grabbed her arm and roughly pulled her to her feet. "Get the hell out of here."

They forced their way through the crush, locating the hallway they needed, but before they could enter it, the lights went out.

"Fuck," Hawk snarled.

Both he and Gray were vulnerable due to a lack of night vision. "I can't see shit," Gray growled.

"Just wait. Your night vision will kick in soon."

"Yeah, if we don't get killed first."

Slowly it came, and Hawk said, "This way."

They slipped into the hallway. A door was open at the other end, letting some light in. "Ilse, where are you?"

"Down here."

A figure appeared in the gloom. "Did you see them?"

"See who?"

"The White Dove and her bodyguard."

"They didn't come this way," Hawk said. He looked at the open door. "They went out the back way. There must be some stairs there. Where is Slania?"

"In here. She needs help."

"Marcus."

Gray slipped past Ilse and went to get the other team member. "Are you okay, Ilse?"

"No, I'm fucking pissed. The bitch got away. Her father is the Silver Fox."

"No use crying over spilled milk now," Hawk said. "Let's get out of here."

Marcus and Slania appeared.

"How's our little Michelangelo?" the former SAS man asked.

"I can still kick your ass," Slania groaned.

"All right, let's go out the back way. Boss, we're on our way to you."

"Copy, Jake."

As they started along the hallway, Hawk said to Ilse, "You know, it was a masquerade party, not a stripper convention."

"Just shut up, Jake."

———

"FIND me what they did with those Africans," Ilse snarled as she entered the old processing factory.

"No," Anja snapped, asserting her authority. "Marcus, treat their wounds. Jake and I will take care of things here."

"Yes, boss."

Ilse didn't like it, but took the order.

With Gray and his patients gone, Anja and Hawk sat at the double console and started looking through everything that they could find.

Anja said, "So we know that the White Dove and Silver Fox are father and daughter. The head of the Chasseurs is Declan Hunter. That is a good intel-gathering mission in my book."

"The Chasseurs must have a base of operations close by," Hawk said. "It won't be at Hunter Enterprises. It has to be a facility outside of the city. Somewhere big enough to keep their hostages."

"I don't think so," Anja said.

"Boss?"

"Throw the net wider. If you were kidnapping

multiple girls at a time and selling them, would you keep them in your own backyard?"

"You're right. I should have thought of that. They'll still need a staging area in the city."

"I'm working on it. There were no cameras within a three-block radius of the auction site."

"Let's look for transport. A van or a small truck," Hawk said. "They will want to get them out of Paris using the shortest route possible."

"From the site, there are only two possibilities," Anja said. "Divide and conquer."

———

SLANIA WINCED. "Easy, stud, that's sore."

The bruise on her ribs was coming out already. Gray nodded. "I don't think you have anything broken."

He turned away to Ilse who sat on the raised bed in her underwear. "Now, let's get you stitched up."

There were four cuts that needed attention. Two required closing. Gray broke out the kit he needed and said, "I'm sorry, I don't have a local."

"Just get it done. Girls are tough. We have babies."

"Yeah, I'll not begrudge you that," Gray said as he prepared everything. "This will hurt though. Either way."

"We need to find them again," Slania said. "I need to kick that big bastard in his oversized balls."

"How do you know they're oversized?" Ilse asked, wincing as the needle pierced her skin.

"I had a handful of the bastard's just before the lights went out. I bet that bitch doesn't keep him around just for his size. Wait, maybe she does."

Ilse chuckled. It was the first time since their return. However, it didn't last long when the needle bit again.

Meanwhile, Slania was now fully clothed and said, "I'll go and see how the others are progressing."

"You should get some rest," Gray said. "You took a beating. Drink some water."

"I'll rest later."

———

"GOT IT," Hawk said. "Small refrigeration lorry. I've tracked it to this location."

Anja got up from her seat and stood behind Hawk. "What is that?"

"It's a sawmill," Hawk said.

"And that is where they went?"

"Yes."

Slania appeared. "Have you found anything?"

Anja nodded. "This sawmill...I need all the intel you can get on it. Jake and Marcus will be going in at first light. I will reach out to Interpol."

"What is the mission, boss?" Hawk asked.

"Secure the hostages and get them out. Once you are clear, then I'll clear Interpol to go in."

"Do you think they'll wait?"

"They'll wait. Now, get some rest."

———

THE TWO OPERATORS MANAGED A COUPLE HOURS' sleep before they were roused. Ilse woke Hawk. "Jake?"

"I'm awake," he replied.

"It's time to get ready."

He rubbed at his face to clear the cobwebs. "On my way."

"There will be a full package briefing in ten minutes."

Ilse made to leave, but Hawk grabbed her arm. "How are you feeling?"

She touched his hand. "I'm good. Focused on the mission."

"I'll get them back," Hawk said. "Count on it."

She kissed his forehead. "I know, Jake."

Hawk and Marcus were ready for the briefing on time. They were already kitted up and ready to go when Anja began:

"Slania will give you the details."

"You guys are going to love this," she said. "The sawmill is backed onto a pine forest twenty kilometers from where we now sit. There are various outbuildings and equipment sheds."

Hawk and Gray looked through the folders. Gray said, "So, we infil through the trees."

"That would be the obvious route. However, if you look at the screen, you will see..."

"Crap," Hawk muttered. "What are they?"

"Laser-activated minefield."

"Rules that out."

"On the contrary, it is the perfect way to go. They won't be expecting it."

"Stealth is of the utmost importance," Ilse said. "You will be equipped with subsonic rounds. The quieter, the better."

"How about only one of us go with subsonic just in case we need the extra punch?" Hawk suggested.

Ilse looked at Anja. She nodded. "Up to you, Jake."

"I'll take the subs," Gray said.

"Fine, let's continue."

Slania said, "Getting through the minefield will be made easier with your laser enhancement glasses. Just don't trip one because I guarantee you, they will all be interconnected."

"They would be. How many guards?"

"Maybe a dozen or so," Slania said. "It varies. The problem is, you're going in in the daylight."

"Where do they keep the hostages?" Gray asked.

"Judging by the heat signatures in this building,"—the screen changed and a photo of what appeared to be a storage building flashed up—"I managed to get clustered heat signatures from it."

"You're sure it's not a barracks of some kind?"

The picture changed again. "Not with these guards out front."

"Backup?" Hawk asked.

"None," Anja said. "You get found out, you fight yourself to the hostages and secure them. Only then will Interpol intervene. We need confirmation."

"Call sign?"

"Lion One."

Gray held out his fist to Hawk. "Go hard."

Hawk returned the fist bump. "Go *fucking* hard."

CHAPTER EIGHT

Paris, France

SVETLANA ANSWERED her cell as she lay in the large bed. She was naked except for the white patches that covered the sutured cuts on her person. Her hair was pulled back into a long braid. Beside her lay Vadim. He, too, was disrobed. On his body was a pattern of purple bruises.

"What is it?" Svetlana asked.

"It's me," Declan Hunter said. "I hope I didn't wake you."

She looked at Vadim, his body bathed in a sheen of sweat. "I've been awake for a while."

"Good. I have your purchase at my facility. We managed to get them out before things got too out of hand."

"I will come and collect them this afternoon," Svetlana informed him.

"They will be ready."

"How did they find you, Declan?" she asked.

"I don't know. Our chain is tight."

"Not tight enough," Svetlana said. "Do you know who they are?"

"I have no idea," Hunter replied.

"They are called Talon."

"The ones who destroyed Medusa?" Hunter sounded surprised.

"Yes, creating what we all are today. They will not stop so they must be killed."

"Meanwhile, business must continue."

Vadim's fingers trailed up the inside of her thigh. Svetlana sighed. "Yes, it must. We have a new business venture opening soon in Moscow. We need something special for the launch."

Hunter thought for a moment. "I think I have just the something you need. Are you familiar with Ricardo Widmer?"

"Shipping magnate in Geneva?"

"Yes. His daughter is having a birthday in a few days. A gala is being held for her twenty-first."

"Do you have a picture?"

"Give me a moment."

While she waited, Svetlana felt Vadim's fingers slide higher. She turned her head to look at him. His eyes were fixed upon her face. The cell in her hand vibrated, and Hunter said, "You should have it."

Svetlana looked at it and was satisfied. "Yes, I think so. How much?"

"Ten million."

"It is a little high, Declan."

"I think she is worth the price tag," Hunter replied.

The White Dove thought briefly. "Go ahead."

"I will have a team in place soon."

The call disconnected, and Svetlana was about to toss the cell and climb onto her bodyguard when it buzzed again. She sighed in frustration. "Hello, Father."

"News has reached me that you had an issue at the auction last night."

"Nothing I couldn't handle."

"Did you make purchases for our business?"

"Yes, Father. I have also ordered another for the opening of our new venture."

"Really. What about those people?" her father asked.

"They are from Talon."

"I see. When will you be home?"

"Soon," Svetlana replied. "After that I have more business to attend to."

"I will see you then."

"Goodbye."

The call finished and Svetlana rolled toward Vadim. "Now, where were we?"

―――――

HAWK STOPPED and adjusted his glasses. Before him lay about twenty meters of spiderwebbed lasers crisscrossing through the trees. They had already come that distance. Somewhere a crow cawed in the trees, maybe expecting one of them to screw up.

Gray led the way through the field. He said, "My nerves will be fucked after this."

"*Yours* will be? Alpha Three, how are we looking?"

"All clear, Bravo."

They pushed through the pines, the smell of damp earth and the sap filling their nostrils. After what felt like hours of painstaking progress, they reached the edge of the trees and paused. Hawk removed his glasses and swept the surrounding area over the barrel of his weapon. There was a clearing of around ten meters before they would find cover in an outbuilding.

Hawk said, "Okay Marcus, let's go to work."

Gray brought up his 416 and stepped out into the open, sweeping left and right. He made it halfway before Slania said, "Target left, Bravo Two."

Settling his sights on the guard's chest, Gray stroked the trigger, and two subsonic rounds put him down.

Moving forward, they reached the first building and skirted around it.

"Bravo Two, incoming at your one o'clock."

Gray turned slightly and waited.

"Two, he has been joined by another X-ray. Confirm two X-rays coming toward you."

"Roger that," Gray whispered.

As the pair walked into view, Gray centered on the first, let out a breath, and then fired. The man started to buckle at the knees. Before he touched down, Gray fired at the second guard. The initial shot missed, but the second hit. Gray muttered a curse and fired a third.

"Careless, old chap," Hawk whispered.

"Screw you. He moved."

Moving off once more, the shed soon appeared in front of them. They crouched down and surveyed their surroundings.

Hawk said, "Alpha Three, what do you see?"

"All clear, except for the two guards at your twelve."

"Roger that. Marcus, send it."

Two heartbeats, two kills.

Pressing forward, they came to the door on the old shed. Reaching out, Hawk tried to open it. "Locked."

Looking down at the dead guards, Gray bent to search them, finding a key in the pocket of the second of the two. He passed it to Hawk who put it into the lock and turned it. With a final look around, Hawk opened the door, and they both slipped inside.

The interior varied greatly from the outside. It was

clean and like a big dorm. The strange part was that all the occupants were lying on a bunk asleep.

"What the fuck?" Gray muttered.

Hawk hurried to the nearest one and checked the woman over. He then moved on to the second and did the same. "They're all drugged."

"Bastards."

"Alpha, copy?" Hawk said.

"Copy, Bravo."

"Confirm that the hostages are on-site. They've all been drugged but they seem okay."

"Roger that. Will let Lion One know. Stand by."

"Copy. Standing by." Hawk turned to Gray. "Marcus, check outside."

Gray moved to the door and opened it a crack. "Still looks clear, Jake."

"Three, sitrep?"

"All clear so far, Bravo," Slania replied.

"Bravo, this is Alpha One. Lion One is five mikes out. Get ready for extract."

"Five mikes, Marcus, let's get ready to receive."

Gray dropped out his partly used magazine of subsonic rounds and worked the charging handle to eject the one in the breech. Then he grabbed a fresh magazine of standard issue and reloaded. With a round in the breech, he was ready to go.

"Bravo One, this is Lion One, copy?"

"Copy, Lion One."

"We are four mikes out. One helo and five vehicles."

"Be advised, Lion, that the packages are all drugged. They are non-ambulatory."

"Understood. Non-ambulatory. Be there soon."

"Also, there are still hostiles on the ground. Anything that moves and doesn't wear a dipshit smile is fair game."

"Roger."

"Are you saying I have a dipshit smile?" Gray asked.

"If the shoe fits."

"Bastard."

The raid went over without a hitch. The Interpol teams assaulted, and the surprise was complete. The remaining guards were captured, and the hostages taken into care. For once, an op had gone off according to plan.

––––––––

"JULIEN MOREAU HAS JUST SURFACED," Ilse told Hawk as he lay on the sofa watching the television. It was early in the morning the day following the raid, and he was relaxing while waiting for new intel.

"Good, I was starting to get sick of watching French television."

"Meeting in twenty minutes."

"Roger that."

Before she left, she bent down and kissed Hawk on the lips. He looked up at her.

"What was that for?"

"Just because. It could be a while before I get to do it again."

"However long it will be, lass, will be too long for me."

"Where did you steal that from?" Ilse asked.

"Read it somewhere," he replied with a grin.

"I thought so."

Twenty minutes later, the team was gathered for the mission briefing. Once they were ready, Anja began. "Interpol made an intercept of a call between Igor Stanislav and Julien Moreau. Stanislav as you know, is an arms dealer. Moreau is after weapons for a rebel faction in Sudan. They were able to put an electronic tag on his cell, and at this very moment, we are tracking him."

"Where is he?" Hawk asked.

"The Grand Palais. You roll in two minutes. I want him alive, Jacob. Nothing else will suffice."

"We'll get him, boss."

"I'm glad you said *we*, Jacob, because I am going with you. Marcus will drive. Ilse will run the operation from here."

Hawk opened his mouth to protest. "Boss—"

"Not a word, Mr. Hawk. I'm going and that is final."

"Yes, boss."

———

PULLING the van to a stop beside the curb, Gray turned off the motor. Anja and Hawk put their earwigs in, and while they checked their sidearms, Anja said, "Comms check, Alpha Two."

"Read you, Lima Charlie, ma'am."

"Bravo One, comms check."

"Roger. Comms good."

Gray said, "Bravo Two comms check."

"Comms clear, Bravo Two."

With their weapons and comms ready, Hawk and Anja slid open the side door and climbed out of the van.

Anja said, "Where is our target now?"

"There is a small building that was built on the southeast side of the Grand Palais," Ilse said. "It is part of the museum. He is in there."

Hawk looked to the southeast. "Did you say small?"

"Copy."

"Yeah, I think you're looking at the map upside down."

"Say again?"

Hawk said, "Boss, don't let me go in there."

Anja held out her arm. "Take my hand Jacob, we'll do this together."

"Lovers again, huh?"

"Exactly. Alpha Three, kill all the cameras within a three-block radius. The only person I want with any kind of eyes is you."

"Yes, ma'am."

"Let's go."

The new building was of sandstone block construction. Anja and Hawk walked up the steps hand in hand until they reached the oversized hardwood doors. The sign on them said closed.

Anja said, "Three, confirm Moreau is inside."

"Affirmative, Alpha One."

"You wearing protection?" Hawk asked.

"Yes, are you?"

"Been shot too many times not to," he said stoically and opened the door.

The entry area was huge. Marble flooring extended to a large water feature with lush greenery and a waterfall. On the left, a grand staircase led to an open mezzanine floor above. Additionally, a more modest staircase on the right led down to another display area. Hawk swept left and right with his P320. "Three, do you have eyes on the package?"

He is up on the mezzanine, sitting in front of some wall paintings."

"Sitting?" Anja asked.

"Has not moved."

"This is a trap," Hawk said.

"I agree," Anja replied. "Bravo Two, be alert. This could be a trap."

"Roger, boss."

Hawk started up the staircase to the landing at the top. The display appeared to be dedicated to mammals. Some of the featured creatures were new to him, but he concentrated on the job at hand. Throughout the open-plan mezzanine were a myriad of pillars and false walls.

Anja was close behind Hawk as they started toward the area where they would supposedly find Moreau. Hawk passed through an area of ruins which looked to be dedicated to ancient Rome. There were a few busts sitting on pedestals and bits of broken and cracked pottery.

"I don't like this, boss," Hawk said. "This is worse than stealing a bloody expensive car."

"Just don't break anything. Okay?"

"I'll do my best."

Ancient Rome gave way to a room containing art where the paintings hung on a scattering of false walls. It was beyond one of these that Moreau was seated.

Hawk was the first to see him, sitting on a jacquard tub chair, his back to them. Hawk pointed his P320 at Moreau and said, "Stand up and turn around really slow, mate."

"It took you long enough to get here," Moreau replied. "Svetlana assured me you would be here, however."

"Who is Svetlana?" Anja asked.

"Oh dear, maybe I said too much."

"I knew it was a trap," Hawk growled. "Three, full sweep of the area."

"It looks all clear—ah shit."

"Shit is never a good word to use in a sentence."

"They looped my loop and blocked what I can see except for you."

"What do you mean?" Hawk asked.

"Don't worry, just know that you are not alone. Take Moreau and get out."

Hawk hurried forward. "Cover me, boss."

Anja pointed her weapon at the back of Moreau's head while Hawk moved around in front of him. Confirming that it was indeed Moreau, he said, "Get up."

The man refused to move. Instead, he looked up arrogantly and said, "I think I'll wait."

Hawk hit him in the face. Hard enough to hurt, but that was all. "You either get the fuck up or the woman behind you will put a bullet in your head and we will walk away."

"Oh, bother. Whatever. You will never get out."

Gunfire ripped through the mezzanine floor, and holes were chewed through some of the paintings hanging in that room. "Shit," Hawk snarled.

He grabbed Moreau in a powerful grip and dragged him to his feet. The man resisted, and this time, the Talon operator slammed his handgun alongside the man's head. "Fucking move. Last chance."

Anja turned toward a staircase in the rear corner of the room. Standing near the top step was the shooter, his weapon raised to shoot. She opened fire with her handgun. Four shots. Three hammered into the wall, but the last punched the shooter back. As he fell, she said into her comms, "Ground team is taking fire. Repeat, we're taking fire. Moving to extract."

Another assailant appeared on the stairs, replacing the one that Anja had shot. He opened fire, forcing them into cover behind a false wall. Of little consequence to the bullets, the wall began to shred, blowing plaster dust and debris all over them with every round. Hawk felt one hit him, but the mix of the wall and the Synoprathetic suit made it feel like little more than a solid punch.

Anja heard him grunt. "Are you all right?"

"I'll live. Let's keep moving."

Using the rapidly disintegrating wall for cover, they moved back through the Rome area. As lead hornets chased them, the fragile pottery around them began to shatter. They took more substantial cover behind some large pillars. Next to Hawk, a bust smashed, shards flying in every direction. He looked across at Anja. "See, this is why we can't have nice things."

"Shut up, Jake."

Hawk turned Moreau around. "These friends of yours don't care who they shoot. You're a means to an end. Remember that."

It suddenly dawned on Moreau that Hawk was right. They weren't worried about hitting him, as long as they got their targets.

Hawk shoved him. "Move."

For the first time, Moreau didn't resist.

By the time they reached the mammal area, there were more shooters coming up the main staircase. Hawk forced Moreau down behind a giant prehistoric wombat. Bullets peppered the dead animal with shattering ferocity. "Shit, boss. As if the poor bastard wasn't dead enough."

Anja was crouched behind another fake animal neither of them had seen before. She dropped out a spent magazine and reloaded then looked around the side and saw a familiar figure.

"Jake, she's here."

Hawk looked for himself and saw her. The White Dove, armed with what looked to be an AK-12. "The bitch means business."

"They have us pinned."

Hawk reloaded, thinking about their next move. His face grew grim, and he shook his head. "Fuck it. Hey, boss?"

"What?"

"You any good at swimming?"

"I was age champion at school. Why?"

More bullets punched into the prehistoric wombat. "Just curious."

Suddenly, it dawned on Anja what he was getting at. "No, Jake."

"The only way, boss."

"We don't know how deep it is."

"I guess we'll find out," Hawk said as he opened fire again.

"Damn it," Anja growled and then leaped to her feet. "If I die doing this, Jake, I'll make sure you pay."

Hawk fired off another six rounds and glanced in Anja's direction just as she went over the edge of the mezzanine. He then grabbed a handful of Moreau's coat, and said, "You hesitate, and you die."

They came to their feet, Hawk dragging Moreau with his left hand while firing the rest of the magazine off with the right. Moments later, they were freefalling from the mezzanine toward the water below.

The pool wasn't deep, but it took the pace out of their fall so that when they hit the bottom, it wasn't much more than a gentle nudge.

Hawk overcame the shock of the impact and straightened up, dragging Moreau upright. "Move. Follow the woman."

Another shove and Moreau was lurching after Anja who was out and firing her weapon at any target she could see. Hawk reloaded, bullets from above splashing all around him. Just as he raised his P320 to fire again, Anja cried out and spun around, falling to the hard floor.

Firing at the shooter, Hawk said, "Boss, are you okay?"

"Fuck that hurts."

"Push through it. It gets better."

Hawk followed Moreau out of the water, and they crouched behind some fake rocks. "Bravo Two, can you hear me?"

There was no response. "The comms are fried. Keep going out the door. Ready?"

"I think I have a busted rib," Anja said.

"Getting shot will do that."

"It wasn't getting shot, it was that bloody kamikaze fucking leap, dickhead."

"Look at the bright side," Hawk said, firing at another target. "You're still alive."

"Just get moving."

The three broke cover, and ran toward the door. They flew open under the blow of Hawk's shoulder, however, the solid impact with the wood sent a giant shockwave reverberating through his body. Bright sunshine assailed their eyes as they burst into daylight, causing them to squint. From out of the glare roared a van, tires screeching as it came to a stop.

Hawk opened the sliding door, and they all scrambled in. He slammed the door behind them, and Gray floored the gas pedal. "Is everyone all right?"

Anja glared at Hawk. They were all wringing wet with water running from their clothes. "We're fine," she said. "For the moment."

"What did you do, Jake?" Gray asked.

"Nothing too bad. Just proved to the boss that she could fly if she put her mind to it."

Gray grinned to himself. Then he said, "Back to the crib, boss?"

"No, to the plane. Let Ilse and Slania know to pack it up. I want to be airborne as soon as possible."

"Roger that."

———

SVETLANA WAS ANGRY. Watching her quarry evade them by jumping from the mezzanine into the pool below was bad enough, but then they ran out the doors and got away in a van. With Moreau. "I want to know where they are going," she growled.

"It might take some time," one of her men said.

"I don't care. Just find them."

"I guess the plan didn't work as well as it could have," Vadim said.

"Really?" Svetlana asked sarcastically, her eyes blazing with fire.

They climbed into their vehicles, taking their dead with them. There was no issue about being identified, for they had taken measures.

Still, Svetlana's anger boiled down deep. How could they have escaped the trap? And to lose Moreau. He was meant to have been killed along with the mercenaries. He was a liability they could have done without.

Her cell rang. It was Declan Hunter. "What happened?"

"I don't want to discuss it," Svetlana replied.

"I take it not well, then?"

"You could say that. Listen, I need to go home for a few days. I'm guessing that you can handle that other thing we discussed?"

"No problem."

"Thank you." The call ended, and Svetlana stewed some more.

CHAPTER NINE

ILSE AND SLANIA were already at the airfield when the others arrived. They parked the van off the apron where it would be picked up later. Their dark SUV was placed aboard the Airbus A400M Atlas. As soon as it was secured, the copilot came down and talked to Anja. "Ma'am, where are we headed?"

"Just get us in the air, Jack, I'll let you know more when we have it."

"Yes, ma'am."

Anja turned to Hawk. "We need to question Moreau."

"Bit hard to do it on a plane with all the noise," Hawk pointed out.

"Put him in the SUV."

Hawk and Marcus grabbed Moreau and pushed him into the rear of the vehicle. Ilse, Hawk, and Anja climbed in and turned to face him. The Frenchman stared back at them, one at a time. "Do you think you can untie me?"

"Yeah right," Hawk replied with a snort.

"I am not going anywhere, I'm on a plane."

"Do it," Anja said.

Hawk let him loose. "Try anything and this thing will need detailing to get rid of your brains."

"What do you want to know? But first, what is in it for me?"

"You get to stay alive," Anja said.

"You will let me go?" Moreau asked hopefully.

"No. There will be other people who want to talk to you."

The plane's hold grew dim as the ramp came up. The loadmaster turned the lights on, and they felt the plane start to move. Outside, Hawk saw the loadmaster discuss something with Gray, who nodded and came over to the SUV's door. He opened it and said, "Boss, we've been cleared to take off. Until you tell the pilot where you want to go, he's going to put us in a holding pattern to the south."

"Thank you, Mr. Gray."

The door closed, and Hawk said, "You called the woman Svetlana."

"Yes."

"She is the White Dove?"

"That is what they call her."

"What is her full name?" Ilse asked.

"I don't know. I only know her first name."

"Are you lying to me?" Ilse asked.

"They were going to kill me. If I knew, I would tell you."

"The big guy with her?"

"Vadim?"

"Yes, if that is his name. Who is he?"

"From what I've been able to gather, he was once Russian Special Forces. Like all the people who work for her."

"He's her bodyguard?" Ilse asked, knowing the answer. She was testing his honesty.

"Yes, among other things."

"Other things?"

"She sleeps with him when she gets bored."

"What is her relationship with you?" Anja asked.

"I set up the auctions," Moreau said.

"For the women?" Hawk asked.

"For anything," he replied. "They are just one facet of what I do."

"What do you know about Declan Hunter?" Ilse asked him.

"Declan is—has a specialty. He's an *acquirer*."

"Just call it what it is," Hawk growled. "He runs a kidnap-for-hire business. And it's global."

"Yes. But he's clever. No one has gotten close except for the masquerade ball."

The plane accelerated along the runway until they felt it start to lift, the turboprops churning at the air outside.

"Where is Svetlana going to go?" Anja asked.

"I have no idea."

"Where was she staying?" Hawk asked.

"You don't think she will remain there, do you? You must be mad."

"You must have some idea?"

"No."

"What about her father?" Ilse asked.

Moreau frowned. "Her father?"

"The Silver Fox. He is her father, yes?"

"I've heard of him, but I don't know."

"Surely you have put it together," Ilse said. "Shit. White Dove, Silver Fox. Both Russian."

Moreau shook his head. "No, I've never thought of it like that. I thought her name came from her silver-blonde hair."

"Shit," Hawk growled. "We know fuck all. Sorry, boss."

"Well..." Moreau started. "What if I told you about a kidnapping coming up...would that help my cause?"

"What kidnapping?" Anja asked.

Hawk reached out and slapped Moreau. "Talk or I'll throw you out of the bloody plane."

"Okay, okay."

"Where is the kidnapping to take place?" Anja asked.

"Geneva."

Ilse waved to Slania. She made her way to the SUV, riding the turbulence as she went. "Tell the pilot we need to get to Geneva."

"On it."

"What are they doing in Geneva, Julien?" asked Anja.

"They are going after the daughter of Ricardo Widmer."

"The shipping magnate?"

"Yes," Moreau confirmed.

"Who? Who is going after her?"

"The Chasseurs."

"Fuck me," Hawk muttered. "How are they doing it?"

"There is to be a gala for her birthday," Moreau replied. "They are going to take her from there."

"When is the gala?" Ilse asked Moreau.

"The day after tomorrow."

Anja said, "We don't have much time. Have Interpol pick him up when we touch down. We have a lot to organize."

———

BY THE TIME the plane touched down, agents from Interpol were already waiting to take Moreau into custody. Glad to hand him over, the Talon team drove off to their new residence, one of three safehouses in Geneva owned by MI6.

It was located in the part of the city that was old, filled with cobblestone streets, narrow alleyways, and historic buildings. The terraces, constructed from stone, were picturesque and held a certain charm.

Settling in, the team got set up and discussed their plan of attack.

"Should we tell Widmer what we're doing?" Hawk asked.

Anja shook her head. "We can't risk him blowing it. Best to ask forgiveness."

"What is the girl's name?"

"Agatha," Slania said. "She is coming up to her twenty-first birthday."

"Do you think you can find her, Slania?" Anja asked.

"Shouldn't be a problem."

"Good. Ilse, Jake, I want you to sit on her just in case they try to move before the party. The rest of us will work the problem."

Slania said, "I'll send you the coordinates of where she is once I find her."

Ilse smiled at her. "Thanks."

Making sure they had their weapons, they headed down the stairs and onto the street, climbing into the SUV. Ilse's cell pinged, and she looked at the screen. "That didn't take long. She is at a coffee shop three blocks from where we are."

Hawk started the motor. "Let's go."

———

THE COFFEE SHOP was on a corner. The large windows had two street frontages, giving a good view inside. There were numerous booths and smaller two-seater tables. Agatha Widmer was in a booth with a couple of her friends.

The girl had long red hair and freckles. Her skin was pale and her smile broad. Hawk sipped his black coffee and placed the cup on the table. "I haven't picked up anything positive yet."

"That is a good thing," Ilse replied. "I have nothing either."

People came and went. At one point, two men entered, and Hawk thought they might have something, but they left after getting takeout coffees.

The waitress returned to their table and refilled Hawk's cup. Her long dark hair hung loosely around her shoulders, and her baggy dress could not hide an athletic figure. "She is pretty," Ilse said.

Hawk looked at her suspiciously. "I hadn't noticed."

"What? You don't notice a pretty young woman when she is right in front of you?"

"I don't know how to answer that," he replied.

"It isn't a trap, Jake. I just made a comment that she was pretty."

He sipped his coffee. "Okay, so she was pretty."

"Prettier than me?"

"I knew it," he said, rolling his eyes.

Ilse smiled. "I'm just joking with you. Trying to break the monotony."

"How is the boss's rib?"

"Broken."

Hawk nodded. "She said it was. She'll need to take it easy."

Agatha and her friends were on the move, rising from their booth and going to the counter to pay before walking out the door, deep in conversation. Hawk handed some cash to the cashier and waited for change, while Ilse left the café to tail the young women. Hawk caught up with her a little farther along the street.

A tram rumbled past them as they walked, its bell

dinging. Waiting as the girls crossed a street and looked in the window of a clothing store, the pair crossed while the young women pointed out different things in the window display before heading inside.

Hawk and Ilse followed them. Hawk realized his mistake when he stopped inside the door. "I don't want to be in here."

Ilse smiled. "Embarrassed?"

"It's a bloody lingerie store. It—" He stopped when a tall blonde approached them. Her blouse was open a couple buttons too many, and her black lace bra barely contained the swell of her breasts. "Shit."

"Can I help you?" she asked with a broad smile.

Ilse shook her head. "We're just looking. Something special."

The store assistant pointed toward a corner and the racks there. "You'll find special there."

"Thank you."

Glad to turn away from the assistant, they walked toward the indicated racks, and Ilse pretended to be looking through the items.

"What do you think?" she asked, holding up an item on a hanger.

"Shit, woman, what do you call that?" It was like a one-piece bathing suit made of mesh with frills at the edges. Without a doubt it would have been totally see-through. "A fish could escape that. I could see all your tattoos through that. And look, someone forgot to sew it up properly down the bottom."

"That's the idea, Jake."

"How much is it?"

Ilse looked at the tag. "Three thousand."

His eyes went wide. "Bloody hell."

There was a giggle from nearby, and Ilse saw that the girls were holding up pairs of lacy bras.

"Did you find anything that you liked?" the store assistant walked up behind them and asked. "We have some wonderful fabrics."

"Or lack thereof," Hawk said.

Ilse nudged him. "Take no notice of my husband."

Hawk pointed at the item that Ilse was holding. "Tell me something, would you wear that?"

"Oh, yes, I have two of them. My husband loves the easy access it provides—"

"Okay, I get it, I asked the wrong person." Hawk looked at Ilse. "I'll be outside."

"Don't you want to help me pick something out, darling?"

"Wait until autumn. Three leaves should do the trick. They would cover more."

Keen to make his escape, Hawk left the store and stood on the sidewalk outside the delicatessen next door. Glancing around, he picked up the dark blue Mercedes across the street.

"Ilse, I have a blue Mercedes across the street that looks suspicious."

"Copy. I'll be out in a moment."

When she came out of the store, Hawk turned his back to the vehicle. Ilse kissed him and wrapped her arms around him as well so that when she embraced him she had a better view. "You think they're Chasseurs?"

"If I had to put money on it."

"What do you think we should do?" Ilse asked.

"There seems to be two options and the first one doesn't count. Either we go back in there and warn her, which lets them know someone tipped her off, or we go over there and take them out and scare the rest away."

"So we let it play out and don't intervene unless we have to."

"That's about it."

They stayed together for a few more minutes before moving to a bench seat conveniently placed on the sidewalk. They waited there until the girls emerged and started along the sidewalk away from the store. Hawk said, "I'm going back to get our wheels. We'll need them if something happens."

"Okay. Just stay on comms."

Hawk disappeared and Ilse kept following the girls. They stopped at a handbag store further along and spent twenty minutes inside. The Mercedes moved accordingly. Hawk arrived while they were still inside. He remained in the SUV while Ilse was in the store tracking the target.

"Jake, do you like Louis Vuitton?"

"You don't earn enough, lass," Hawk replied.

"I've found a nice bag here for twenty-seven hundred Euros."

"I don't see the money in things like that, I really don't," Hawk said in disbelief. "All they are is a carry-all for junk."

"There is a lot more to them than that," Ilse pointed out. "A woman's life goes into one of those."

"Can't it fit into one that costs ten quid?"

"You are a neanderthal."

When Ilse emerged, she was carrying the bag. Hawk shook his head. "What did you do?"

"I needed to buy something to look the part while I'm following them. I put it on the company card."

"Anja will have a cow."

The three friends emerged from the store and turned in the direction they had originally come. Once they reached the coffee house, the girls climbed into an Audi. After following on foot, Ilse joined Hawk, who had gone around the block in the SUV, while the two in the Mercedes performed a U-turn.

Agatha and her friends, oblivious to their tails, drove

to a terrace apartment three blocks away. After parking on the street, they went inside and stayed there.

Ilse called Anja. "Do you have any connections in Geneva that might watch the girl around-the-clock until the gala tomorrow night?"

"Is there a reason for around-the-clock surveillance?"

She told her about the Mercedes and its occupants. "All right, stay where you are. I'll see what I can get for you."

An hour later help arrived in the form of two men not unfamiliar to the Talon operatives.

The rear doors opened, and both men climbed in. "Someone said you needed help."

Hawk didn't even turn. "Should I shoot you now or later?"

John *Grizz* Harvey smiled. He was a big man, about six-five. "Is that any way to greet an old friend?"

"John, Linc," Ilse said.

Linc Sheffield nodded. "Ilse, Jake."

"It is good to see you. I didn't know you were in Geneva."

"Working a detail. We had some spare time, and when the boss called, we decided to help out. So, what are we doing?"

Ilse filled them in. "Only intervene if there is immediate danger to life."

"Roger that."

"Stay out of trouble," Hawk said.

"The name is John, not Jake."

———

THE HELICOPTER LANDED in a cloud of dirt and snow. As the rotors wound down, two figures emerged from within. Once they reached the door to the castle, each went their separate way.

Svetlana's shoes clicked on the flagstone floor, traversing the vast hallway, making several turns before entering the great hall. She found her father seated in front of a large open fire.

"You have returned, my dear," he said without turning around.

"I said I would, father," Svetlana replied, bending to kiss his forehead.

"How was business?"

She walked to the end of the mantel where the drinks were and poured a glass of vodka. "Let's say that business wasn't as fruitful as I had hoped."

He detected a hint of bitterness in his daughter's voice. "I take it that the thorn in your side has become a knife?"

"It is nothing I cannot handle."

"I seem to have heard that before," her father said, raising an eyebrow.

Svetlana finished her drink and poured another. Her father stared at her. "You seem to have a few more scars and bruises."

"That knife you were talking about."

He nodded. "Sit."

His daughter took the bottle and flounced dejectedly in the chair next to her father's. Its softness wrapped around her and helped her relax. "Declan is acquiring something special for our Moscow venture."

"Yes, you told me. How special?"

"Ten million."

"I see. What about the auction?"

"You already know about that."

"Tell me in more detail, Svetlana."

He'd used her name. A sign he was becoming impatient. She relayed exactly what had happened, omitting no detail. Then she added, "We set a trap for them at the museum in Paris."

"I have heard."

"You seem to hear a lot of things. Maybe I should purge my team and start again. Get people I can trust."

"That won't be necessary. What are you going to do?"

"I have to go to Berlin tomorrow on business. To see an investor for the upcoming meeting you insist on having here. From there, I head to Rome and then Venice."

The Silver Fox held out his glass, and Svetlana filled it for him. "The investors are important for the new venture in Moscow. I need them all here so I can convince them that I need their money more than they do."

"So you can seduce them with whores and alcohol."

"Whatever works, my dear, whatever works."

Svetlana sat and stared into the fire, watching the flickering flames. Then, after a long period of silence, she said, "I need your help, Father."

The Silver Fox nodded. "I think you do."

CHAPTER TEN

THE AFTERNOON OF THE GALA, they sat around a table and discussed what was going to happen that night. Anja said, "Jake, I managed to get you in as a security person. That means you'll be armed, which is good. Ilse and Marcus will be serving, while I have managed to score an invitation as a guest. Slania will be running our operations from a van parked outside. Simple, really."

"Nothing is ever simple, boss," Hawk said. "How am I meant to be security when they will have their own people?"

"The boss of the security company is an old friend from my intelligence days. He was French intelligence. I told him of the threat and convinced him not to put any more people on duty. We can't have the Chasseurs forewarned."

"You do realize that this could go very loud very quickly."

"I am aware of that fact. It is our job to make sure that it doesn't. Familiarize yourselves with the building. Know all the exits and rooms you can use to help in any way. You will also be carrying concealed weapons. Just in case."

"Boss, if this does kick off, what is the procedure?" Gray asked.

"Jake will get the package to safety while the rest of us will try and see that he is able to do that."

"Where is safety?" Hawk asked.

"Get her in the van and Slania will get you out of there. The rest of us will find our own way. The girl is the mission. Understood, Jake?"

"You know, I get the feeling that certain people around here blame me when things go wrong."

"I wonder why?" Ilse commented.

"Are there any further questions?" Anja asked.

They all shook their heads.

"All right, let's get ready. Oh, and try to take at least somebody alive."

THE BALLROOM WAS COLOSSAL. It was adorned with intricate furnishings and lifelike artworks on the wall. The ceiling had a large mural painted on it and a large hand-carved roses surrounded the chandelier fixtures.

Hawk shadowed the birthday girl wherever she went and was able to do it with ease through the crowd. Meanwhile, Anja mingled with some of the guests, and Ilse and Gray went about their waiting duties.

All of them were hooked into comms and had small hidden cameras on their person.

"This kid gets more presents in one night than I get in a bloody lifetime," Hawk muttered into his comms.

"Feeling jealous?" Anja asked.

"Not in the least. I just wish she would slow down a little."

"Too much of a social butterfly for you?" Slania asked.

"I don't know about butterfly. She gets around like a peregrine falcon."

"Do you see anything, Slania?" Anja asked.

"Nothing suspicious yet, boss. Unless you consider Jake stuffing his face every few minutes in that category."

Hawk snatched something off a tray going past, one that crunched when he bit into it. "Hey, you try keeping up with this girl on an empty stomach."

Ilse broke into their chatter. "Jake eats more than a horse. I swear he has a big tapeworm somewhere inside him."

"It's good nosh," Hawk said.

"Mind on the job, Jake."

"Yes, boss."

They were an hour into the gala when things changed.

Gray noticed that one of the waiters had different shoes to the rest. He frowned, looked around the room and noted that there were more waiters present than had been earlier. "Three, can you get some facial rec on the waiters?"

"Do you have a problem, Bravo?" Slania asked.

"I've got a waiter with different shoes and there seem to be more of them in the ballroom than earlier."

"Give me a moment," Slania said, and then she went quiet.

"Three, are you okay?"

"Wait one, Bravo Two."

"What's happening, Three?" Anja asked.

"Boss, I have got a catering truck pulling up—okay, that is not good. Boss, there are armed men climbing out of the back. This is it."

From her observation position, Slania saw them making for the front door. "They're coming in the front. They just shot the guards on the door."

"Check the back," Hawk said.

There was a moment of radio silence, and then she said, "There are more around the back."

"Right." Hawk hurried over to Agatha and her friends. "You, come with me right now."

"What? Who are you?"

"No time for that. Move." Hawk gave her a shove.

"What the—"

Gunfire ripped through the ballroom. Hawk pulled his weapon and said, "Come on."

He took her by the arm and forcefully dragged her toward a staircase. As he went, he said, "I have the package. Headed for the upper floor."

Ricardo Widmer appeared in front of them. "Where are you taking her?"

"Up," Hawk replied. "There are more of them coming in the back."

Widmer looked at his daughter. "Go with him. He will keep you safe."

"But, Papa."

Then he was gone.

"Come on, girl, let's move."

———

ILSE EXTRACTED her P320 from its hiding spot and prepared for contact. Like the others—except for Anja— she was wearing her Synoprathetic suit beneath her waiter's uniform.

A shooter appeared through the surging crowd. A vigilant security guy tried to be brave and take the weapon away from him. The killer knocked him to the ground and put two bullets into him.

The P320 in Ilse's hand sighted center mass, but her shot was blocked. She waited, the line of sight cleared, and Ilse fired.

The prospective kidnapper fell to the floor, unmoving. Gunfire erupted somewhere else in the room. "Boss, where are you?"

"At your twelve," Anja replied.

Ilse saw her then. She was bending down to collect the shooter's weapon. It was an FN P90 submachine gun. She also grabbed a spare magazine. Another assailant appeared to her left, so she brought the P90 sweeping around but held her fire. A terrified woman running toward Anja blocked her view. "Get down!" Anja shouted at her.

The woman's fear was too great, and she just kept coming. The kidnapper fired, and the look of fear on the woman turned to shock. She fell forward and crashed to the floor.

"Fuck," Anja cursed and fired the P90.

The kidnapper fell.

"We have to try and get these people out of here," Ilse said. "Marcus, where are you?"

"Kitchen."

"Are you okay?"

"I'm holding my own."

Suddenly, Slania came over their comms. "We've got more inbound."

Anja's face grew grim. "Ilse, Marcus, on me. Now."

————

HAWK PUSHED Agatha up the stairs in front of him when the first smoke canister went off and started to fill the ballroom. Gunfire seemed to be everywhere. He cast a glance back over his shoulder and saw a kidnapper at the bottom of the stairs. "Bollocks."

Hawk aimed his P320 at the man and fired three rounds. Behind him, he heard Agatha cry out in alarm.

Hawk spun around and saw another kidnapper at the top of the stairs. How the hell...

The Brit opened fire, and the kidnapper staggered back. Agatha tried to turn and retreat down the stairs. Hawk grabbed her and said, "No, get back up there."

Her protests fell on deaf ears. Hawk forced her onward, stepping past the fallen man when they reached the top of the stairs. Turning right, they hurried along a wide gallery, a red carpet runner extending its length. Hawk picked a door and tried it. The handle turned, and the door snicked open. The only thing in the room was the furniture. Hawk pointed at a chair. "Sit there."

The sound of distant gunfire filtered up from the ballroom. Hawk locked the door. Agatha looked to Hawk for guidance. "What are we going to do?"

"Keep you safe, lass," Hawk said, looking around. "That is what this is all about. Get under the desk."

"What?"

"Get under the desk. If someone comes through that door shooting, I don't want you catching a stray bullet."

"I will not—"

"Get under the bloody desk, damn your eyes. I told your old man I would keep you safe and—"

The door flew open, and a shooter appeared. This one was different. He wore body armor and an ice hockey mask. The mask narrowed his vision, and he didn't see Hawk. The Brit threw himself at the intruder and crashed into his side.

The intruder grunted under the force of the unexpected impact. The pair crashed to the floor. Hawk ripped the mask free to get access to the person's head. His balled fist stopped mid-swing when he recognized it as a woman. "Fucking bollocks."

The woman took advantage of his hesitation and hit Hawk with an elbow to the jaw. It hurt, his eyes watered and he rolled away from her. The woman, still on her back, made a play for her sidearm.

Hawk had dropped his and was forced to roll to one side to retrieve it. He scooped up the P320 and opened fire.

It had all taken time, and the woman fired first. Her bullets fanned his face, and one tugged at his suit coat as it passed through. Hawk blew off three rounds in return. The first two took the woman in the body armor. The last in the head.

Hawk took a deep breath. "Fuck!"

He came to his feet and rushed to close the door. Agatha was still standing there, frozen in terror. "Bollocks, girl, get under the bloody desk."

This time, she did as she was ordered.

Hawk hurried over to a large double window. He opened it and looked down. It was too high for them to jump, but to the left was a downpipe. "That'll do."

He turned back to the room. "Agatha, come here."

Now more subdued, the girl crawled out from under the desk and over to where Hawk was. "We're going down the pipe."

She gasped. "In this dress?"

Looking at it, Hawk nodded. "You're right. Get it off."

"You're joking."

"You don't understand, do you?" Hawk growled. "These people are here for you. They will kidnap you and sell you into prostitution. But if all you are worried about is a little modesty, go right ahead and stay."

Agatha ripped the bottom of her dress away and hurried toward the window. "Good girl. Slania, copy? First-floor window. Coming down the pipe. We may need some help."

"On my way."

While Agatha started out the window, Hawk said into his comms, "Sitrep, boss?"

"What is it that you military men say? SNAFU?"

"I just say it's fucked," Hawk replied.

"Yes, it's fucked."

———

ILSE GOT SHOT TWICE. WHAP! WHAP!

The pain was intense. "Shit, fuck."

It was a good thing she had her Synoprathetic suit. Although the material might have been bulletproof, but it still hurt like a bitch to get shot. Gray came out of the smoke at her side and pulled her to her feet. "Come on, lass, up you get."

"That hurt," Ilse growled.

"Always fucking does."

A shooter appeared in body armor and facemask. Gray sprayed the figure with five rounds from his P320. The shooter staggered and went down onto a knee. The former para stepped forward, dislodged the mask and shot the man in the head. "Things just got even more intense, boss. It's time to get out of here."

"Where did they come from?" Anja asked, knowing what he was talking about.

"No idea."

"We can't leave them all," Ilse said.

"Jake has got the girl. She was the mission. We stay here much longer, one of us will get killed. Get out, now. Interpol have a response team on the way."

"Roger."

———

AGATHA STARTED down the stormwater pipe. Hawk stood near the window covering her retreat. He heard voices coming closer to the room. The position he was holding was too vulnerable, so he jumped back into the room and hurried toward the door, locating himself beside it, and waited.

Two figures in full body armor entered. Hawk fell in behind the first one and shot him in the back of the head. The second he pressed the P320 against his neck and said, "Drop your fucking weapon."

The man's assault rifle fell to the floor with a clatter.

"Walk toward the window and stand in front of it."

Once the man was there, Hawk removed his mask and said, "Coming down, Alpha Three."

"What?"

Hawk hit the man with the butt of his handgun and pushed him at the same time. The body toppled forward like a large tree and disappeared out the window.

"What am I supposed to do with him, Jake?" Slania asked.

"He's a present for the boss."

Agatha was almost down, and Slania was waiting for her. Hawk started down as soon as her feet touched the garden bed below. He slid down and turned to see Slania escorting Agatha to the van. Staring down at the unconscious Chasseur, he shrugged and said, "I guess you're mine."

Hawk grabbed the man by the collar and started dragging him toward the van. Grunting with the effort of picking up the dead weight, he threw the body in the rear of the van and climbed in.

"Boss, where are you?"

"One mile out. Get ready to go."

Moments later, they appeared. Hawk was relieved

that they were all fine. They climbed into the van and Ilse settled in beside Hawk. "Are you okay?" he asked.

"I got shot twice."

"Hurts, huh?"

"Shit yeah."

Slania started to drive. Anja pointed at the figure on the floor. "Who is that?"

"Present."

"Just what I wanted."

————

THERE WERE twelve casualties from the gala. However, Agatha's father and friends had made it out. Most of the dead and wounded were staff and security. Meanwhile, Agatha had been picked up by Interpol and whisked away to a secure location.

However, at their secure location, the Talon team still had their Chasseur to question. Anja and Hawk took the lead.

A small interrogation room with cameras and microphones seemed crowded with its three occupants. It was cold and concrete and inhospitable.

Anja said, "I'm not going to ask you your name. I tend to forget them anyway after they're dead."

The man gave her a curious look. "What?"

He was British.

Anja continued. "Don't worry, I won't be the one."

He looked at Hawk. "Don't worry, mate, I'd like to, but the boss won't talk to me for a week if I did that. No, your own people will be the ones."

"My lot won't kill me," the man said indignantly.

"They will when they find out you sang like a bloody canary."

"But I haven't."

Anja smiled. "Not yet."

"If you want anything out of me, then I need protection," the man snapped.

"There it is," Hawk said. "Sometimes it doesn't take much."

Anja leaned across the stainless-steel table. "Talk. Tell us about the Chasseurs."

"What do you want to know?"

"Okay. Is Declan the boss?"

"Yes."

"Where are they based?"

"The Czech Republic."

"Why there?" asked Hawk.

"Since the new government took over, they tore up all the extradition treaties."

"So that is where their headquarters is?" Anja asked.

"Yes."

"And you can show us on a map?"

"Yes."

Anja stared at the two-way mirror. Ilse was on the other side and would get the message.

"What was the plan for Agatha?" Hawk asked.

"She would be shipped to our base and passed on from there. She was a special order."

"For who?"

"Svetlana."

"The White Dove?" Anja asked, wanting to confirm.

"Yes."

"Why not France? Wait for the auctions."

"They never have auctions in the same country twice in a row. Declan has operations everywhere."

Ilse knocked before entering the room. She had a map rolled up and placed it on the table before leaving. Anja unfurled it and said to their prisoner, "Show me."

The man looked at the map and stabbed it with his finger. "There. An old castle."

"What does Declan keep there?" Anja asked.

"He has a book. A ledger, if you like. It details everyone who he has sold to. You get that and you're halfway there."

"The Silver Fox?" Hawk asked. "Is he in it?"

The prisoner shook his head. "I don't know. The only way to find out is to get it."

"Where is it kept?"

"In a safe in the library."

"Tumbler? Digital? Both?" Anja asked.

"Digital."

"Combination?"

"No idea."

"Where is it? The safe?"

"No idea."

"Are you certain the ledger is there?" Anja asked again.

"Positive," the prisoner replied.

———

"I GUESS we're going to the Czech Republic," Hawk said once the team was gathered around the conference table.

Anja nodded. "Even if we don't get information on Svetlana or her father, we'll be able to make a start on dismantling the trafficking pipeline."

"How are we going to do it?" Gray asked.

"Our friend pointed out where the library is in the castle. We do it discreetly until we can't anymore," Anja replied. "Get in, get the ledger, and get out. We need that intel."

"Did the girl get away all right?" Hawk asked.

Ilse nodded. "Yes. She and her family are in hiding.

She said to say thank you and if you ever tell anyone you saw her ass, she will hunt you down and kill you."

"She had underwear on."

"From what I saw when she was coming down that pipe," Slania said. "It wasn't covering much. I don't know how women can wear those things. Nothing worse than a thin strip of fabric digging into your ass crack."

Hawk and Gray were trying not to laugh. Ilse and Anja even cracked a smile. Then Anja said, "Are we done?"

"Yes, boss."

"Good. Get some rest. We've got work to do."

CHAPTER ELEVEN

DEEP WITHIN A DECIDUOUS FOREST, the castle sat surrounded by lakes. In the fall, the woods were a myriad of colors, from orange, to red, to yellow. But this time of the year, they were green with new growth. Not that Hawk and Gray could tell because it was dark.

In full combat kit, complete with NODs, they had their suppressed H&K 433s. Insertion had been across a lake via a motorized inflatable raft. Making successful landfall, it was a matter of using the tree for cover to get close to the castle.

Once in position, Gray put up a small drone no bigger than the palm of his hand. As it launched, he said, "Alpha Three, drone away."

"Roger, Bravo Two, acquiring the Insect now."

Slania gained control from her position in the truck with the others who were watching the mission on screens.

The Insect took to the sky and flew toward the castle. It hovered above a parapet and scanned the immediate area. "All clear, Bravo. Proceed."

Hawk and Gray came out of the trees to the base of

the castle wall. Once there, Hawk unshouldered the grapple gun and aimed it at the parapet.

"Sitrep, Alpha Three."

"All clear."

The gun fired, sending the hook flying up over the wall, trailing the rope behind it. Hawk pulled it back to make sure it was locked into place. He took the powered ascender out of his pack and started up the wall.

His rifle was slung, so he held on with his left, and in his right was his suppressed SIG. As he crested the parapet, he swept left and right, clearing the immediate vicinity.

Gray was close behind and soon joined Hawk on top. Both men lifted their NVGs. "Holy shit," Gray whispered.

"You got that right, Marcus me lad."

The photos didn't do the castle justice. It was immense. What they were on was the outer wall. Inside was the main building. Four floors which resembled a large hotel.

Hawk said, "We'll circle around the wall before we get down."

Setting off along the parapet, they kept watch for possible threats, and soon found the stairs. They descended the stairs stealthily, taking cover in the darkness of the shadows at the base.

Hawk said, "How are we looking, Alpha?"

"There is a side door on the left of the main building. You can get in there and have access to a stairwell."

"Roger that."

"Hold position, Bravo," Slania said hurriedly. "You have an X-ray coming toward you from your right."

"I have him," Hawk whispered.

The man walked past with what seemed to be casual strides. Hawk waited for him to disappear before stepping out of the shadows and heading for the main building. The rough stone of the building appeared to be centuries old, but without time to enjoy the history, they moved on. Reaching the door, Gray extended his hand and tried the knob, the catch snicking open.

Hawk said, "Bravo, now breaching."

"Copy, Bravo."

Once inside, they found the staircase like Slania had said they would. Hawk began to ascend ahead of Gray.

Hawk and Gray reached the first floor and stopped. Hawk checked the door. It opened slightly, and the former SAS man peered through. The long stone hallway was clear. He noted the wall lamps and the four doors on either side of the hall. "Alpha, which one are we looking at?"

"Second on the left. I have no heat signatures in it. However, the first room on your right has two distinct signatures."

"Copy."

Hawk and Gray pushed forward along the hallway as quietly as possible until they reached the door. It was locked. Gray stood post while Hawk took out his lockpicks and went to work. Moments later the door was open and they slipped inside, closing it behind them.

"Now, all we have to do is find the ledger," Gray said, flicking on his flashlight.

"Check for a wall safe first," Hawk said.

Pulling back each picture to check behind them, they found nothing. It was then they turned their attention to the two large shelves of books. They had only just started when Slania said, "Bravo, we have a rover traversing the hallway."

Hawk and Gray turned off their flashlights and listened in silence as footsteps walked along the flagstone floor. There was a pause, and then the walker kept going.

"Keep searching, Bravo. Your friend has moved on."

A few minutes later, Gray said, "I've got the safe, Jake."

Hawk hurried over to his friend. Gray had his flashlight shining on the electronic keypad. "Alpha Three, we have the safe."

"Tell me what you see, Bravo."

"It's not your normal keypad. It has numbers, letters, and Roman numerals."

"What is the make? Does it say?"

"SchlossWache."

"Okay, give me a moment. Yes, right. Lever the cover off the pad."

"Roger," Hawk whispered and took out his knife. He pried the pad cover off and the whole pad itself came away. "Oops."

"What do you mean oops?" Anja asked.

"The whole pad came away and we're left with wires."

"Cut them," Slania said.

"What?"

"Just cut them away, you don't need the pad. But you will need to hurry because once you cut them, a silent alarm will be triggered."

"Great."

"Is there any way to stop it?" Gray asked.

"No, it's built-in."

Hawk muttered something incoherent.

"What was that?" Gray asked.

"I said fuck, I love this job. Let's do this."

Hawk cut the wires and dug out the electronic reader he was carrying. He started to hook it up, and Slania said, "Alarm has started. Marcus, there is already movement coming your way."

"Roger that," Gray said and picked up his 433 from its strap. "I got this, Jake."

134

Gray raised his suppressed weapon and pointed it at the door. His comms came alive. "Here they come. Two of them from the room across the hallway."

The door flew open, and Gray fired. The first man through went down in a howl of pain. The former para sought the second shooter and found him. He fired, and bullets tore through the man's throat, spewing forth a spray of arterial blood.

"Two X-rays down." Gray glanced back over his shoulder. "Come on, Jake, open the damn thing."

"Just waiting on the machine, mucker."

Hawk had hooked up the decoder, and it was scanning through its code. Moments after he had replied to Gray, it beeped twice, paused, and then beeped again. "Done."

The former para turned the handle, and the safe swung open. It was full of papers and other items. Hawk opened his backpack and started shoveling everything in. At the bottom of the safe's detritus was the ledger. Hawk opened it and had a quick scan. "Alpha, I do believe I have the package. Moving to extract."

"Not before time. The castle is coming alive, and I have a mobile convoy coming in from the east along the road."

"That's bullshit," Hawk said. "No one could react with vehicles that quickly."

"Unless they were expecting you or they were already on the way," Anja said.

"I'm guessing the latter. Shit." Hawk looked around. "The window."

"Shit, we're always going out fucking windows," Gray replied.

Moving quickly to the window, they disengaged the lock. Hawk pushed it wide and leaned out. There was nothing between them from the window to the garden. "We're going to have to jump."

"What is it they say? Tuck and fucking roll."

Voices sounded from the hallway. Men appeared and filled the void. Gray took cover behind the desk and opened fire. "Get out, I'll be right behind you."

"Make sure you bloody are," Hawk growled and climbed out.

Gray opened fire, and the first of the Chasseurs fell to the floor. His partner took cover behind the doorjamb before returning fire with a long burst.

Bullets ripped into the desk and sent splinters scything through the air. Wicked, razor-sharp missiles which could slice flesh to the bone.

"I'm down, Marcus," Hawk said over his comms.

"On my way," Gray replied. "Keep clear."

"What are you—" Gray had already run at the opening by the time Hawk had started his sentence. By the time he stopped, Gray had already jumped through the opening and was on the way down. "You stupid fucking pillock."

The former para landed hard in the garden. He let out a moan and rolled over. Hawk grabbed his hand and helped him to his feet. "Dickhead," Hawk growled. "This way."

They had only moved a few steps when two guards appeared. The guards opened fire, and Hawk and Gray ran to their right to look for cover. As they went, they opened fire, trying to deter their attackers.

Hawk stopped suddenly as bullets sliced all around him. He took deliberate aim with his 433. Then he stroked the trigger, and the shooter dropped to the damp ground.

The second shooter was joined by two more. "Oh shit."

They opened fire, and Hawk felt the strike of a bullet in his armor. He staggered and went down. "Fuck."

A hand grabbed him roughly and pulled him to his feet. "Come on, you."

Gray helped him up, and they lurched away.

"Alpha Three, we need a way out," Hawk said breathlessly.

"Go up, Bravo. Get on the parapet."

"Roger."

Both men headed up a set of external stairs. Behind them, they could hear shouts and bullets still peppering all around them. Then things changed again.

Someone turned on the floodlights.

Then the explosions started.

"Fuck," growled Hawk as he started up the stairs. "They're firing cannons at us now."

"It's coming from the convoy, Bravo," Slania said. "Looks like they're coming in hot."

Hawk and Gray crouched down on the steps amid the incoming fury. Hawk shouted at his friend, "Keep moving! Push up!"

They kept climbing to the parapet as more of it was destroyed. Then suddenly, the stone stairs gave way from a hit near the base. With a cry of alarm, both Hawk and Gray tumbled down.

They hit hard among the debris, pain shooting through their bodies. Over their comms, Hawk heard Slania say, "Talk to me, Bravo."

"Two operators down."

"Hang on, we're on our way."

And then the visitors arrived.

———

IGOR GROMOV LOADED a magazine into his AK-12 and toggled the transmit button on his comms. "We are

137

almost there. There will be no survivors. We make an example of the mercenaries."

Gromov knew they were coming. The Silver Fox's intelligence web had managed to gather that information. The lights of the castle appeared before the five-vehicle convoy through the trees.

Atop one of the parapets, Gromov could see the winking flashes of gunfire. He said, "I need a report on what is happening."

"The situation is fluid, Comrade," a voice from one of the other SUVs said.

"Well, fucking unfluid it."

"It looks like the targets are making for the south parapet."

"Put fire upon it now."

The third vehicle in line was a Humvee. On top was a mount that fired grenades at sixty rounds per minute. A heartbeat after the order came, it opened fire.

———

ANJA GRABBED her body armor and her weapon. "Ilse, with me."

Ilse grabbed her own equipment and followed her boss out of the truck. "Slania, we need real-time updates."

"Roger that, I'll keep you covered."

They ran toward the castle and the sound of guns. The rate of fire sounded intense. They reached the wall where Hawk and Gray had gone over. Anja and Ilse grabbed their powered ascenders and were soon going up the wall. As they climbed, Slania said, "Looks like the lads have dug in among the rubble."

Anja grunted. "Bravo callsigns, report."

"Just peachy, boss," Hawk replied. "Could swap fire with our friends all day."

"Sarcasm does not become you, Jacob," Anja said.

"I don't know. I thought it was one of my finer traits."

"Just give me a sitrep, Bravo One."

"We're banged up but we're holding our own. If you can lay down some fire from the parapet, we might—we might be fine. But you need to watch that fucking grenade launcher."

"Roger that."

The two women topped the parapet and crouched to survey the scene before them. It was a chaotic firefight of bullets and explosions. "Fuck," Anja growled. "Ilse, the grenade launcher. Now."

Ilse's 433 had its own HK 269 grenade launcher. Slipping a grenade on while down on a knee, she fired it.

The explosion took the Silver Fox's mercenary team by surprise as the vehicle with the automatic grenade launcher exploded violently. Ilse reloaded and fired another grenade at a second vehicle.

The vehicle suffered the same fate as its predecessor in a ball of flame. Now, the shooters in the courtyard changed their points of aim and concentrated their fire on the parapet.

Both women dived to their stomachs as the incoming rounds became more intense. "That got their attention," Ilse said.

"Bravo, get out of there while you can," Anja barked.

"Roger that. Moving now."

———

HAWK SMACKED Gray on his head. "Come on, Mucker, time to move."

"What?" Gray spun his head to look at Hawk. There was blood running down the side of his face from the hairline.

"Shit," Hawk growled. "Time to move."

"Roger that. You know you're bleeding, right?"

Hawk touched his cheek and felt blood. "I'm not the only one."

They came out of the rubble of the destroyed staircase and ran toward one further along the wall. Twin fires burned among the vehicles, and rifles winked as they continued their rapid fire.

There wasn't time to stop and fire. The situation called for head down, ass up stuff and get from A to B as fast as possible. Hawk and Gray reached the stairs and started to climb. Anja and Ilse were now back on their game and laying down more covering fire.

The two Bravo men ignored their pain and managed to reach the parapet and run along it to where the women were busy. They crouched next to them, and Anja said, "Get over the side."

"Yes, boss."

"Have you still got the ledger, Jake?" Ilse asked.

"Roger that."

Hawk and Gray went over the wall while Anja and Ilse lay down heavy fire. Ilse still had grenades to throw out, and she created carnage upon the Silver Fox's minions. She turned to Anja. "Get gone. I'll be right behind you."

Anja commenced her descent while Ilse let loose a long burst with the 433 and fired her last two grenades to keep heads down. Then, she followed her commander over.

"Alpha Three, we're coming to you. Be ready."

"Three standing by."

Ilse jumped to her feet and turned to run to the ledge. She took two steps when she felt a blow to her back. It felt as though she had been kicked by a horse, but the Syno-prathetic suit held.

Thrust to the parapet floor on her stomach like a giant hand had pushed her over, Ilse lost grip on her weapon as she impacted the stone. It skidded from her grasp.

"Alpha Two, where are you?" Anja asked.

The force of getting shot had knocked the air from her lungs, and even as she tried to talk, she found she couldn't. A croak was all that escaped her lips.

"Say again, Alpha Two."

"I'm d—down."

———————

"FUCK," Hawk snarled. He turned back to the wall.

Anja blocked his path. "Jake, I'll go."

He handed the ledger to Anja. "Get this out of here. This is what I do. No one left behind."

"I'll give you a couple of minutes. We won't wait."

"I don't expect you to." Then he was gone.

He still had his ascender and hooked it to the rope. Holding his 433 in one hand, he let the machine carry him up. As soon as Hawk topped the parapet. He saw two Chasseurs. His finger depressed the trigger, and the 433 came to life.

The Chasseurs jerked wildly under the bullet impacts and fell dead. Hawk unhooked himself and ran along the parapet. He dropped out the almost-spent magazine and replaced it with a fresh one.

Seeing Ilse ahead of him and no present threats, he crouched beside her. As he did so, another Chasseur appeared. The 433 spewed rounds, and the man disappeared over the edge of the parapet. Ilse moaned. "Where are you hit, old girl?"

"My back."

"Have you got a suit on?"

"Yes."

"Then you'll be fine. Get up."

"Thanks for the sympathy, asshole," Ilse growled.

"There's the lass I love." He grabbed her clothing. "Come on, we've got a ride to catch."

Another moan escaped her lips as he helped her up. "I wish the company would invent something that didn't hurt as much when you get bloody shot."

"Let's you know you're alive."

He helped her over the parapet and began her descent. Moments later, Hawk was behind her. When they reached the bottom, they swiftly detached, and the pair disappeared into the trees with bullets chasing them.

———

IGOR GROMOV WATCHED the two enemy combatants escape into the forest. He muttered a curse and then pointed at the two men beside him. "You and you. Get some people and find them."

The mercenaries disappeared, leaving the Russian on his own. He already knew they would be too late. A few minutes later, Declan Hunter joined him.

"That went well," Hunter said with more than a hint of sarcasm.

Gromov turned and stared at the Chasseurs boss. "Who are these people?"

"I did some digging after the first incursion. They are called Talon. They are a splinter group from the Global Corporation."

"I wish someone had told me that before."

Lightning flashed to the east, the product of a brewing storm. Thunder rolled across the landscape as though it was admonishing Gromov for his failure. The Russian shook his head. "Fuck it."

CHAPTER TWELVE

"THE LEDGER IS BLOODY USELESS," Hawk growled, throwing copied papers onto the table in front of him.

Ilse frowned. "It won't have it in lights saying, 'Look at me,' Jake. You have to read between the lines."

"That is why I kick doors, and you do the smart stuff," Hawk said.

"Look at the third page, boss," Ilse said.

Anja flicked through the papers and found what she was looking for. "What am I seeing?"

"Down toward the bottom. There is a name. Geier. Recognize it?"

"Oh, yes."

"Who is this Geier?" Hawk asked.

"Geier is German for *Vulture*," Ilse supplied.

"It is also German for *arms dealing*, asshole," Anja said.

"I'm guessing that this is important?" Hawk asked.

"When we were with German intelligence," Ilse said, "we came across him in Bosnia trying to sell decommissioned Russian weapons. Except they weren't decommissioned, they were stolen contemporary weapons. Including a tank."

"He gave us the slip and went to ground. But the man is a wealth of knowledge. He's grown in reputation since then."

"What's the plan?" Hawk asked.

Anja sighed. "There is nothing in here about Svetlana or the Silver Fox. This was a waste of time. We need to find a reliable source."

"We're giving up on Hunter?" Hawk asked.

"On the contrary. We pick him up and interrogate him for everything he has. But first, we have to find him. Geier will help us with that." Anja turned to Slania. "What can you tell us?"

"Satellite feed had Hunter at the castle the other night. With this guy—Igor Gromov. He was part of the reaction force. Or ambush if that takes your fancy."

"Tell me about Gromov," Hawk said.

"He is former Russian Special Forces. Retired colonel. Since then, he's been virtually invisible."

"A lot like his boss, I'd say," Hawk said. "I'm going to hazard a guess that he is a Silver Fox man, not White Dove."

"Extra help?" Ilse asked.

"Could be."

Anja nodded. "What happened to Declan Hunter?"

"Vanished as expected."

"Right. We concentrate everything on Geier. Where can we find him?"

Slania smiled. "Berlin."

———

THE VULTURE, A.K.A. Mesut Kahn, sat in the back of the strip club, smoking an opium pipe with a young escort on either side of him. In the next booth were three men. His bodyguards. Across the table sat a Russian national who was looking for weapons to supply to a rogue general in Mali.

"You want me to pay an exorbitant price for weapons from my own country?" the man asked.

"You came to me," Geier said.

"Yes, but six hundred million Euros?"

"They will need to come in two shipments," Geier said. "That is a major reason for the expense."

"When?" the man asked.

"Three months."

The Russian almost fell off his seat. "Three months? The coup will be over by then."

"I can't help that. I'm a busy man."

"I will have to consult the general," the Russian said.

"You know where to find me when you decide."

Getting to his feet, the man looked at the arms dealer for a moment before being joined by two bodyguards at a nearby table, who followed him out. Geier watched them leave. Reaching out, he grabbed his glass of vodka. He took a sip while one of his lady friends leaned in and nuzzled his neck. He ran his hand up the inside of her thigh until she allowed him to move it all the way and touch the thin fabric of her underwear.

He started to rub his fingers in a circular motion, but she stopped him. "Not here, Mesut. Wait until later."

"What? Where is your sense of adventure?"

The young woman smiled widely, showing her whitened teeth. "What I have planned for you is only fit for the privacy of our suite."

Sudden movement across the table snapped his attention from his companion as two people sat down. A man and woman. The man he'd never seen before. The woman he knew intimately. Five years earlier, German intelligence had been tracking him. This was the woman leading the charge.

"Anja Meyer, it has been a little time since our last interaction."

The two ladies beside Geier already felt the tension rise. Anja nodded. "I'd prefer that you were dead, Mesut, but I guess for what I want, this will do."

"Who is your friend?"

"His name is Mr. Put a Bullet in Your Fucking Brain."

"Such a mouthful. What happened to that lovely one you worked with? I had such fantasies about you."

A topless waitress arrived with drinks and leaned across the table in front of Hawk. In his ear, he heard Ilse say, "Concentrate, Jake."

The waitress left and Anja indicated Ilse sitting watching from another table. "She is over there. There are more, so if your bodyguards get anxious, things could get very ugly."

"What do you want?"

Hawk looked at the women. "Take a walk."

Both slid out of the booth and moved away. The bodyguards started to move. Hawk produced his P320 and placed it on the table. Geier glanced at his people and shook his head. They sat back down.

Anja said, "Declan Hunter. I want to pay him a visit."

"So?"

"I want to know where he is."

"I don't know," Geier said.

"Are you sure, Mesut?" Anja asked. "See, you are one of the few people in Europe who knows everything. Come to think of it, you might even know these names. White Dove and Silver Fox."

A pained expression came over the arms dealer's face. "Don't."

"So you do. Where are they?"

Geier shook his head. "No. I'm not telling you anything about them. You can have Hunter. He's hiding in Romania at an old Russian nuclear missile facility."

"The Russians never had a nuclear missile facility in Romania," Anja replied.

"If you say so. It is in the Carpathian Mountains. Beside a lake up there. You can't miss it."

Anja stared at him. "Now, what about the others?"

"I will not sign my death warrant for you or anyone else," the Vulture stated. "Just know this. The Fox is up to something big in Moscow."

"What, Geier?" Anja demanded. "What is he up to? Is it his trafficking of women?"

"That is the Dove."

"Svetlana?"

"So, you know her name. Yes, she is the trafficker. She is the one who works with Declan Hunter. Her father, sure he uses some of the girls she supplies to make his supporters more pliable, but he is way beyond that."

"Give me his name, Mesut," Anja said.

He shook his head and opened his mouth to speak. It was then that a bullet ripped through the air and into his open maw. It blew out the back of his head in a messy red spray. Hawk and Anja spun around just as the strip club was enshrouded in the sound of gunfire.

"Everyone out, now!" Anja snarled, drawing her weapon.

Hawk already had his P320 in his hand. He raised it and aimed at the shooter who had killed Geier. He only had a heartbeat to make a decision, and he made it. His finger stroked the trigger, and the bullet blasted from the weapon across the short distance and punched into the shooter's head. In the time that it took, the round missed a topless waitress by barely an inch.

More weapons fire rattled through the screams, and

Hawk figured someone had a compact submachine gun. He looked for Ilse and saw her disappearing into the crowd. A figure fell in behind her in the confusion and Hawk noted that he held a handgun.

"No, you fucking don't, cock."

Hawk pushed through the scattering crowd and almost tripped over a body at his feet. More gunfire, and a patron in front of him was hit. The man staggered and fell forward. Hawk caught him before he hit the floor.

He stared at Hawk with pleading eyes. "Take it easy, mate. I got you."

The man grunted.

"Ilse, copy?"

"Yes."

"Watch your back. You have a tail."

"Roger—oh fuck." There was a flurry of shots and then Ilse came back to him. "X-ray down."

"Boss, are you good?"

Suddenly, Anja kneeled beside him. "I'm fine, Jake."

"There you are. This poor sod is hit hard."

"Slania, are there paramedics on the way?"

"Yes, boss."

Anja touched Hawk on the shoulder. "Leave him, Jake. We need to leave."

Suddenly, a familiar face appeared over them, a handgun pointed down. Hawk reacted instantly and spun, sweeping the legs of Gromov from beneath him. The Russian cried out in surprise and fell back, his handgun triggered, sending a bullet into the ceiling.

Hawk threw himself at the Russian, but the man was no longer in the same place. Gromov had rolled away and come to his feet like a cat.

Hawk's sudden movements produced an immediate reminder of his recent ordeal at the castle as pain racked his body. Gromov rushed forward, and the Brit met his charge by bringing the P320 around and smashing it into the side of his head.

The Russian collapsed to the floor among the fast-growing debris field. Hawk took a step forward and felt himself thrust to the side as another attacker hit him hard.

"Fucking hell," Hawk growled as he hit the floor once more.

With an animalistic snarl, the Russian mercenary tried to drive a knife through Hawk's throat. Hawk caught the killer's wrist in his free hand and stopped the knife cold. Then he shoved the barrel of the P320 into his ribs and fired four times.

The man jerked and grunted under each hammer blow. Pushing him away, Hawk came into a crouch. He looked for Gromov and found him gone. "Why does everyone want to bloody kill me?"

"I want to shoot you, and I like you," Slania said.

"It's good to have friends who care," he growled.

Standing up, Hawk started toward the door. The shooting seemed to have died down. He said, "Check in."

Ilse and Anja called in. "We're almost out."

"Copy. Gray?"

"Roger, I'm almost out too."

"Copy. I'm on my way."

Beginning his retreat, Hawk moved faster toward the door. He managed to avoid getting shot somehow while killing another two shooters. However, the strip club was a slaughterhouse. Dead and wounded were everywhere. It was the type of scene that would make news headlines across the globe. He just wondered what they would say.

Once outside, they regrouped. Anja was mad, and her emotions showed. But instead of venting wildly, she said, "Come on, let's get the hell out of here."

———

Venice, Italy

In a way, Svetlana was pleased. Pleased that her father's people had fared little better than hers. However, there was a chance that the Talon mercenaries had gotten information out of Geier before her father's people had killed him.

They had not long left the hotel when her cell rang. Svetlana was seated in the back of a black BMW on her way to catch a flight to Berlin to see what needed to be tidied up.

"Hello."

"It's Declan."

"I believe that you've been having problems," she replied.

"Nothing I cannot handle."

"Never mind, you are not the only one these mercenaries are hassling. What can I do for you, Declan?"

"I have a shipment ready for you. Two actually. There is one in Belarus and the other from Romania at Station Thirty-Six. I managed to cobble them together at the last moment."

"I hope cobble doesn't mean what I think it does?" Svetlana asked as the street outside flicked by.

"They will be above standard as always," he assured her.

"I wanted something special for the—well, for my father."

"You shall have it."

Svetlana thought for a moment. "I will be there in a few days."

"Until then."

HAWK PLACED coffees down in front of Ilse, Gray, and Slania. It had been almost twenty-four hours since the shit show in the strip club. Headlines in the Berlin papers screamed terror attack. The number of dead and wounded was unacceptable, and meanwhile, there was no feed from any security camera within or around the vicinity.

Hawk said, "Geier claimed that the Fox was up to something in Moscow and that his daughter ran the trafficking side of things."

Slania nodded. "It sounded important."

"He sounded scared."

"I agree," Ilse said. "But what could be so important in Moscow?"

"I think I might know," Anja said as she entered the room where they were gathered around a table. In her hand were several printed sheets of paper. She put them on the table. "A friend in German intelligence just faxed through this invitation list. Our Silver Fox friend is having a get-together in his nest in the Ural Mountains."

"Does your friend have a name?"

Anja smiled like the cat who had swallowed the canary. "Boris Orlov."

Hawk shook his head. "Shit, how many Boris Orlovs have there been over the years?"

"Our friend is one of the richest oligarchs in modern Russia."

"You seem to be using that *our friend* line a little too freely, boss."

"Just look at the sheet I gave you, Jake. It took me a moment to get it, but an important detail is there."

Ilse glanced up at Anja. "Has this list been verified?"

"Yes," Anja replied. "I knew you would pick it up right away."

"I have it," Slania said.

Hawk threw his back on the table. "It's just all names to me, boss."

"Ilse?"

"All of these names belong to generals, former generals, admirals, Russian air force commanders, oligarchs, and influential politicians."

"Okay. I'm a door kicker. Explain."

"I would say Orlov is planning a coup. Whatever the invitations are for, I would say that is to get them all onside."

"Then we had better interrupt it," Hawk said. "Where in the Urals?"

"That we don't know," Anja replied. "So we stick with the plan. Take Declan Hunter and hope he can point us in the right direction. Slania, I need everything you know about the base in Romania."

"I'll get to work immediately. I should have it within twenty-four hours, boss."

"Thank you."

———

EVERYTHING WAS ready by noon the following day. They were gathered around while Slania briefed them on a big screen.

"This is what the Russians used to call Station Thirty-Six," she started. "It was a missile base in the eighties."

Hawk looked at the overhead shot. There were a handful of buildings surrounded by trees, and at their center was a large circle. "Is that the old silo?"

"Yes."

"It may be a dumb question, but it *is* empty, right?"

"Don't worry, Jake, it's empty."

Gray said, "Now that the dumb questions are out of the way, what forces on the ground are we looking at?"

"A handful, no more."

Ilse frowned. "That seems a low number."

"Most are spread out across Europe. This place is like a small way station. We can expect to find hostages on-site."

"Air cover?" Hawk asked.

"If you want some," Anja replied. "I might be able to get us a new toy."

"MQ-9B SkyGuardian." Hawk sounded hopeful.

Anja nodded. "Global picked up a handful last summer. Hot off the rack. I'll get us a pilot to fly it and Slania can ride second seat."

"Now you're talking my language, boss."

"Okay, continue with the briefing."

Ilse said, "Boss, can we get a mobile command platform from here on out?"

"What did you have in mind?" Anja asked.

"A Marabou?" Ilse suggested.

The Marabou was a newly modified C-17 command platform. With its range it was perfect for the job.

"I second that request, boss," Hawk said. "We can jump into the target."

"What about extract?" Anja asked.

"Across the lake. Can you have a couple of boat teams on standby? Just in case we need to get hostages out."

"Fine. The less time on target, the better."

Gray said, "Just to clarify, boss. If we can't take Hunter clean, do we terminate?"

"Yes. Whatever happens, the Chasseurs must be shut down."

"Roger that."

"When do we go?" Hawk asked.

"Three nights from now."

CHAPTER THIRTEEN

THE GRAVEL ROAD meandered in a serpentine path around the weathered, time-forgotten missile silo buried deep within the earth. The dull crunch of gravel under tires reverberated through the air as three imposing, dark-colored SUVs made their deliberate journey halfway around the inground structure before coming to a halt.

From each vehicle, armed men emerged with military precision. The final figure to step out was Svetlana. Her entrance exuded authority. Dressed in a long, sleek leather coat that flared as she moved, her eyes shielded by dark sunglasses, and her striking silver-blonde hair cascading freely around her shoulders, she was the embodiment of elegance amid the rugged surroundings.

Vadim came around to where she stood and escorted her forward. Hunter stood waiting to greet her. "It is good to see you, Svetlana."

"I will be the judge of that," she replied primly.

"Would you care for a drink before we get started?"

"No. Let's get this done. I have to be back in the air as soon as possible."

"Fine. Follow me."

A building across the way was their destination, and they began walking toward it. There were two guards stationed outside the solid door. Svetlana asked, "Where did you get these from?"

"All were sourced locally except for one," Hunter replied.

"How many are there?"

"Five here and five at the other site. Is that enough?"

"It will suffice. Are they clean, Declan? No prostitutes?"

"One is a secretary, another a blogger, two are lawyers, and finally, the *special one*, is the wife of an Italian fashion designer."

Svetlana stopped. "Are you kidding me, Declan? Lawyers and a wife?"

Hunter turned to face her. "Yes. The lawyers are quite attractive."

"Lawyers are fucking trouble. They are too strong-willed. They need to be to succeed."

"If you don't want them, I can rehome them elsewhere. The Albanians will pay good money for them."

"The Albanians will fuck them once and throw them away. What about the wife? How old is she?"

"Mid-thirties."

"Shit, Declan. Why?"

"Wait until you see her. You'll change your mind."

"We'll see," Svetlana said skeptically.

As they reached the building, Hunter signaled to his men. "Bring them out."

The two guards opened the doors and vanished within the interior's gloom. Moments later, they returned, escorting five women. Each was attired in the clothing which they'd been wearing when kidnapped.

Svetlana ran a meticulous eye over them. It was easy to pick out the two lawyers. They looked more defiant than the others. The wife of the fashion designer was better dressed and had a look of class about her. Svetlana nodded. "I think she will be fine."

"Shall we talk money?"

"Yes. Tell me a figure and halve it."

"I would be prepared to forget the figure, say, if you stayed over for the night," Hunter said.

Svetlana sighed. "As tempting an offer as that is, I must forgo it. My appointment cannot wait."

"In that case, fifty million."

"I already told you I cannot stay, Declan, so stop fucking me," the White Dove said sternly.

"It is a fair price."

"There is nothing fair about it."

"Fine, forty million."

"I will give you ten and not a penny more."

"Now, who is fucking who?" Hunter asked.

"How does it feel?"

"Fine, I will accept fifteen million for these and the others together."

Svetlana nodded. "Then we have a deal. Get them ready for transport while I transfer the money."

———

"BRAVO ELEMENT ARE on the ground and proceeding to the target," Hawk said into his comms.

"Copy, Bravo," Ilse replied from 30,000 feet overhead. "We have you on screen. SkyGuardian is in place and sending back good feed."

The night was cool and the area they had hit when they parachuted in was like a postage stamp. Hawk and Gray were dressed in full combat kit, complete with body armor and NVGs. Their weapons were suppressed, and they also had underslung grenade launchers on their weapons.

Hawk and Gray entered the woods and started toward the old nuclear facility. Somewhere up in the trees, an owl hooded its mournful cry. For the next hour, they use their stealth to get as close as possible. Once they were in position, they paused and watched the facility.

"What do you make of it?" Gray asked.

"Looks reasonably quiet," Hawk replied. "Alpha Three, what do you see?"

"ISR shows a quiet camp. Picking up heat signatures for seven people."

"What about the hostages that are expected to be on site?" Hawk asked.

"If I had to guess, I'd say they're gone."

"Fuck, it's too late. I need a position on our target."

"Wait one, Bravo."

Hawk and Gray crouched beside each other. "What do you figure they've done with them, Jake?"

"Who knows? They could be anywhere in Europe by now. Alpha Two, copy?"

"Copy, Bravo."

"Is there any way we can backtrack and see what happened to the hostages over the past twenty-four hours?"

"Bravo, this is Alpha. I'll have a look, see what I can do. Meanwhile, continue the mission."

"Roger that."

A few heartbeats later, Slania came back online. "Bravo, it looks like your target could be in the building at your two o'clock. It is the only figure that we can pick up on heat signature that is on their own."

"Roger that. Moving now."

Hawk came to his feet and started across the open ground, heading for the first building. Gray was close

157

behind him. Nearing the structure, they slipped into the shadows and waited.

Hawk peered around the corner of the building. Everything looked clear. He was about to go when Ilse said, "Bravo, you have an X-ray approaching from your three."

Hawk let his weapon hang and took out his knife. Remaining still and silent until he saw the figure approaching, he stepped out and struck when the guard drew within reach.

A calloused hand clamped over the guard's mouth, and the knife came up. It slid between ribs with a practiced ease and penetrated the man's heart. Hawk heard the muffled grunt and withdrew the blade before striking again.

Easing the body to the ground in the shadows, Hawk put his knife away. He took his 433 back up and kept moving.

The old site was littered with obstacles. Pipes, crates, and other discarded detritus. There were even old trucks just left there when the site was abandoned. The only things taken by the Russians when they left were related to their nuclear program.

"The building you want is ahead of you, Bravo," Ilse said in his ear.

The two operators crossed the gap and Gray tried the door. It snicked open, and they edged inside. The first room was open plan, set up like a living room and small kitchen. There was a door at the rear of the building which Hawk guessed would lead to sleeping quarters.

Using hand signals, Hawk indicated the door. Gray started across the room and was almost at the door when it exploded outward in a shower of splinters and bullets.

Hawk and Gray threw themselves to the floor. "Alpha

One, Bravo is in contact. I say again, we are in contact. Fuck!"

"Do not kill him, Bravo One," Anja growled.

"Easy for her to say," Hawk snapped. "Marcus, put some fucking fire on that door. Alpha, I need to know what is happening outside before they do."

"Roger."

Gray opened fire on the door to suppress the outgoing. Hawk pulled the pin on a flashbang and ran forward. Gray stopped firing and Hawk threw the flashbang through a jagged opening in the door.

The stun grenade detonated with a loud crash. Hawk kicked the door with his combat boot, and it flew open, making the wall vibrate as it made contact. He entered and found Hunter staggering around in a daze.

"Get down! Get down!" Hawk shouted.

Not comprehending the command, Hunter continued staggering around, trying to regain his composure. Hawk forced him to the floor and restrained his hands behind his back with zip ties, then put a gag on him. "Alpha One, we have the package."

"Copy, Bravo. Good work."

"Bravo, this is Alpha Two. You have multiple X-rays moving to your position."

"Define multiple, Two."

"At this point in time we're looking at ten."

"Shit, that is more than five."

"What can I say. Things change. Deal with it."

"Just drop a bloody Hellfire on them."

"Last resort, Bravo," Anja said. "When we got clearance for the op, we were told in no uncertain terms that the releasing of heavy munitions was to be just that. If things get too hairy, I will release their use. Until then, do your best."

"Do your best? Are you bloody joking, boss?"

"I'm not here to joke, Mr. Hawk. Just like you are here to follow orders." Anja's voice was curt.

"Copy," Hawk said and turned to Gray. "Things are about to get busy. Grab our friend."

Gray pushed Hunter toward the door, Hawk leading the way. Once they reached it, Hawk said, "Alpha, I need a way home."

"Once you're outside, Bravo, go right and circle around to go north."

"The lake is south."

"Do you want to get out of there or not?"

Hawk opened the door and immediately came under fire. He brought up his 433 and returned it. As he burned through half a magazine, he called back over his shoulder, "Keep going, I'll cover you."

Gray pushed Hunter outside and to the right. Hawk filled the void and started firing again. Once the shooters were suppressed, Hawk made his break. The three of them were out of sight now and running toward the cover of another building when all hell broke loose.

Rounds tore through the air like giant hornets. Parts of the building behind them started to disintegrate. Gray threw himself at a door which crashed back, and he fell through, dragging Hunter with him.

Hawk followed them through while the rounds kept up their steady rate of fire. "Alpha, what the hell is that?"

"Looks like there are automatic weapon points, Bravo. Now we know why there aren't too many shooters on site."

"You need to get rid of them or we're going nowhere except into the ground."

"Copy. Standby."

Gray pulled the gag down from Hunter's mouth. "How many do you have?"

"You will never get out of here," Hunter sneered.

Gray punched him in the face while they lay there. "Fucking pillock."

He replaced the gag and looked over at Hawk. "What are they going to do?"

"Fuck knows."

After a few more moments of terrifying firepower, Ilse came over the comms. "Keep your heads down. You've got munitions coming in hot. Three...two...one..."

WHOMP...BOOM!

The Hellfire missile smashed into the automated weapon station, and it disappeared into a ball of flame. The building they had taken cover in shook violently.

WHOMP...BOOM!

A second automated station blew up.

WHOMP...BOOM!

"Bravo, you're all clear. Move now before they regroup."

"Roger that," Hawk said. "Thanks for your assistance. Let's go, Marcus."

They continued their race to get out of the complex and soon found themselves back in the woods. They then began to circle around to the lake where their extract was awaiting their arrival. As they approached, a low voice said, "If your name isn't Hawk, I'll fuck you right up."

Gray said, "Jake, it's your boyfriend."

"Crucible?" Hawk asked, using the codename.

"Roger that."

"Great, let's get out of here." No one moved. "What the fuck are you waiting for?"

"I need the word."

"What word?"

"The password, numb nuts."

"Fuck's sake."

"Try again."

"Shit. Winston."

"Well done. Now, let's go."

SVETLANA GOT the message not long after she returned to her father's base in the Urals. She stared at it for a long time as icy wind whipped through the open courtyard and around her partially clothed body. It was something she did regularly. The cold sharpened her senses and helped her concentrate.

After a moment, her head lifted, and her icy gray eyes stared ahead. There were small flakes of snow on Svetlana's cheeks. She whirled and went inside, her bootheels clunking on the castle flagstones.

Returning to her room, Svetlana showered and then dressed in jeans and a jumper. She knew her father would be waiting for her in the dining hall. As she left her room, Svetlana came across Vadim. She stopped him.

"Vadim, I need you to do me a favor after you've eaten."

"Yes, ma'am."

"Use what resources we have available and find where those mercenaries are. It is time to remove them from our equation."

"I'll see what I can find out."

As expected, Svetlana found her father in the dining hall. He had already started his meal of shashlik which was grilled meat. Svetlana took a seat, and her father's waiter appeared. He set the meal in front of her and removed the cover then walked away. They both continued in silence before her father broke it.

"It seems we have both underestimated the mercenaries."

"They hit Declan Hunter's compound in Romania

and took him prisoner. It was lucky that I wasn't there when it happened and got the girls out before they came."

Orlov placed his knife and fork down. "These people are going to cause me problems, aren't they?"

"I have looked into them. Their main mission is to stop human trafficking. I would say that they know nothing about the other."

"Can you guarantee that, Svetlana?" Orlov asked.

"Can we guarantee anything in life, Father? However, I have Vadim looking for them. Once I know where they are, we will take the fight to them."

"Be careful, daughter," Orlov cautioned Svetlana. "This dog bites. Hard."

Svetlana smiled at him. "So does this bitch."

———

THE MOBILE COMMAND post remained grounded in Poland while they questioned Hunter. He was being held in a facility that Polish Intelligence used for their special prisoners.

Observing the inquisition were two Interpol officers. Delmas and Remy. Delmas was a woman, early forties, blonde, blue eyes, slim build. Remy was male, tall, dark hair, wearing a suit like his boss. They stared at Hunter through the mirror. Delmas said, "The famous Declan Hunter."

There was more than a hint of disdain in her voice. Ilse said, "He is nothing but a predator."

The door opened to the room, and Hawk and Anja entered. Pulling out the chairs opposite Hunter, they sat down. Anja placed a folder on the table. She stared at him for a moment before speaking. "Finally, the empire of Declan Hunter comes crashing down around him."

"What empire?" he asked.

"Let's start with human trafficking, slavery, kidnapping, murder, plus a million other things that Interpol will bury you under."

"I am a telecommunications—"

"Bullshit!" Hawk growled. "You're a fucking scummy murderer and human trafficker. Consider yourself lucky I didn't put a bloody bullet in your head to start with."

"Who do you people think you are anyway?"

"We're Talon, mate. Your worst fucking nightmare."

Hunter snorted derisively. "My lawyers will have me out of here in a heartbeat. Where are they anyway?"

Anja leaned back and folded her arms casually across her chest. "You are going nowhere."

"Nice accent. Let me guess. German?"

"Can I punch him in the face, boss?" Hawk asked.

Behind the mirror, Delmas glanced at Ilse. "Does he mean it?"

Ilse sighed. "I'm afraid he does."

"Must go over well with your commanders."

"We don't have any," Ilse replied.

"What do you mean?"

"We are autonomous. We make our own decisions, run our own budget, and have our own equipment. The only time we reach out to our base is if something really needs to be run up the pole. All decisions are made by us with Anja having the final say."

"She is that capable?"

"Quite. She ran her own team for German intelligence. I was part of it at the time," Ilse explained. "Jake is former SAS, Marcus was a para, and Slania used to be Special Forces Group out of Belgium before going into intelligence. We all complement each other in one way or another."

She saw Remy staring at her. Ilse was dressed in jeans and a T-shirt, which revealed the sleeves of the black body suit she wore beneath it. "It is called a Synoprathetic suit. It is bulletproof up to a certain caliber. It will stop a 7.62 but hit it with a fifty and it'll punch right through it."

"Have you ever been shot while wearing it?"

"More than once," Ilse replied.

"And?"

"It hurts."

Meanwhile, Anja had ignored the question and continued to stare at Hunter. "Mr. Hunter, there is no way out for you. Multiple kidnaps, murders, for all we know you could be involved with terrorist entities. That will get you locked up in a nice deep hole right there."

"That is bullshit," Hunter snapped.

"Jake?"

"She's right, mate, you're fucked. You help us and maybe you'll see sunlight one day."

"When you're two hundred and fifty," Ilse muttered.

"You have nothing on me." It was a stupid statement.

Anja said, "Play the recording."

Soon, the sound of the auction they had infiltrated could be heard over a speaker. Still Hunter wasn't fazed. "That could be anyone who sounds like me."

"Would you like us to show you the camera feed that goes with it?"

He stared at Anja long and hard. He was planning his next move when his world caved in, and his shoulders slumped. Hunter said, "What do you want to know?"

"Let's start with something easy," Anja said. "What is the name of the White Dove?"

Interrogation 101. Start with something you know the answer to and see if the suspect is going to lie. "Svetlana Orlova."

"And the Silver Fox is her father?"

"Yes."

"How long have you been selling women to him?"

Hunter shook his head. "Not him. Her. Svetlana runs the prostitution and escort side of the family business."

"So she buys the girls? Comes to you when she is shopping?"

"Yes. She took a lot the day you came—"

Hawk grabbed Hunter's shirt and would have dragged him across the table if not for his chains. "You sodding bastard. I should have killed you when I found you."

Anja placed a hand on Hawk's arm. "Jacob, let the man go."

Hawk did as he was ordered and leaned back in his seat.

"Now, where were the women taken?" Anja asked.

"I'm guessing to the Fox's den or the compound in Siberia," Hunter said.

"Where is that?"

"Which one?"

"Where will we find Orlov?" Anja asked.

"Somewhere in the Urals," Hunter replied.

"And the women?"

"Those would have gone to the Urals also."

"What was that you said about Siberia?" Hawk asked.

"That's where Svetlana has a base. They take most of the women there and do some mind-bending shit to them. Kind of like memory erasure. I've heard they have a couple of psyche doctors there who oversee the reprogramming before they let them loose."

"Fuck me," Hawk said. "They're worse than Medusa."

"They were part of Medusa until you went and fucked it up," Hunter growled. "Once that happened, they branched out on their own and this is the result. Some of us managed to make a living after that."

"You call kidnap for hire a living?" Anja asked before Hawk lost his cool again.

"You do what you can."

"Do you know where the compound is in Siberia?"

"I can point you in the right direction," Hunter said with a nod.

"Now, tell us about Orlov."

"He's an oligarch with lots of money," Hunter said, acting as though he need say no more.

"I already know that. Tell me something I don't know."

"He used to be SVR after the KGB went tits up."

"And?"

"He still has a lot of friends in the government. Hard-line people who don't like the way things are going."

"So, he's looking to back a coup," Anja said.

"Could be."

"The question is, who is he looking to put in the current president's place?"

Hunter gave a wry smile. Hawk said, "What are you bloody smiling at?"

The head Chasseur replied, "Better the devil you know."

Realization hit Anja. "He's going to do it himself."

———

"WHAT DO WE DO NOW?" Hawk asked Anja now that they were all gathered. Interpol had taken their prisoner, and Talon was working on their next move in a safe-house apartment in Warsaw.

"I need to go away for a few hours," Anja said. "I'll take Marcus with me."

"Where to?" Ilse asked.

"I'm going to have a meeting with a current Russian intelligence officer and inform him of what we have learned."

"Do you think he will believe you?"

Anja shrugged. "I can only try."

"What do you want us to do, boss?" Slania asked.

"Gather all the intel you can on that compound in Serbia. I want to know the place inside out once I get back."

"On it."

"Jake, get us some help for the mission. Can you find us a couple of shooters that you trust?"

"What about hitting up Thurston for a strike team?" Hawk asked.

Anja nodded. "Ilse?"

"I'll get one."

"Fine, let's get to work. We've got twenty-four hours to get this done."

CHAPTER FOURTEEN

WITHOUT HESITATION, she stepped out into the middle of the street and stopped. Traffic was streaming left and right, some drivers honking their horns as they went around her. Then Anja saw what she wanted, bringing up her P320, forcing the vehicle to stop.

"Get out of the fucking car!"

———

ILSE LET the phone ring until it was picked up in England on the other end. "Thurston."

"General, it's Ilse."

"Is everything okay?" Standard question because of what Talon was.

"Yes, General. I'm calling about a favor."

"You better tell me what it is."

Ilse said, "We're in Warsaw. We have a lead on a trafficking base in Siberia, but we need some extra firepower."

"What kind?" Thurston asked.

"A Strike Team."

"Where did you say you were?"

"Warsaw," Ilse replied.

"ST Falcon are in Berlin. I'll have them head your way within the hour. I'll give you a number so you can coordinate with them. Their commander is Lex Tomlinson. His men call him Luthor. It's a four-man team. Is that sufficient?"

"Should be enough."

"Fine. I'll text the number. Good luck."

Hawk was sitting across from her, with Slania working beside him. "All good?"

"Yes. I just have to call the team leader. Lex Tomlinson."

"Never heard of him."

The number came through, and Ilse was about to call it when her cell burst into life. The number was from Gray. Ilse hit the accept button and the speakerphone and said, "What's up?"

"The boss stole a three-million-dollar car!"

Hawk lurched forward. "She fucking what?"

———

THE KOENIGSEGG AGERA streaked along the streets of Warsaw in a flash before Anja was forced to tread heavily on the brakes to make the turn. She glanced at Gray and snapped, "You have a big mouth."

The former para grinned and put the phone on speaker. "—all the times she told me not to steal rides and she goes and does the bloody same thing."

"We don't have time for this, Jacob," Anja called out, going through the gears again.

"What kind?" Hawk asked.

"A Koenigsegg Agera," Gray replied.

"Be fucked. Is it good?"

"If you are quite done?" Anja asked. "Is Ilse there?"

"I'm here, ma'am."

"Evacuate the nest. We're compromised. Meet at the plane."

"Roger that. Are you both all right?"

The car slid sideways around a corner. Gray leaned over and steadied himself against the door. Anja straightened up and floored the gas pedal. The former para said, "If I don't make the plane, it will be because my asshole has gone through my mind after we hit a bloody wall."

He disconnected the call and grabbed the door again as Anja steadied to make another turn. "Holy shit."

Gray looked into the side mirror to see if their pursuers were still back there. When he saw nothing, he said, "You can slow down, boss, there is no one back there."

Anja eased her foot back a little on the gas pedal. She opened her mouth to speak when suddenly a Eurocopter EC635 swept through an intersection in front of them.

"Bloody hell," Gray growled. "There is always a fucking helicopter."

The 635 did a high banking turn and swept back around. It came at them front-on, the 12.7 mm gun pods opening fire.

Large chunks of asphalt kicked up off the Warsaw street as the deathly firing line came at them. Then, just as it seemed the Koenigsegg Agera would be violently torn apart, the intersection was there, and Anja turned hard.

The helicopter pulled up and began to circle back. Behind the wheel, Anja was a picture of concentration.

Gray said, "Boss, make for the anti-noise tunnels."

Anja knew what he meant. The anti-noise tunnels were designed to reduce traffic noise for residents living near busy highways. They were made of glass and steel. But the problem was they were only about 1.2 kilometers long.

Gray knew what she was thinking. He said, "If we get to them, we can get into the traffic tunnels near the river and then we can lose the helicopter."

Anja slowed, swerved around a car, dropped back a gear, and slammed the gas pedal down. The Agera cried out as it was fed a good amount of energy. Gray felt himself pushed back into the seat once more as the speed from the machine elevated.

Meanwhile, the helicopter had circled back around. It was now coming in from the side while the Agera weaved through traffic.

It opened fire. Not at the speeding vehicle Anja and Gray were in, but at the ones ahead of them, going in the opposite direction. Two of the vehicles erupted in flames, swerving across the street. "You sodding bastard," Gray growled.

Anja gritted her teeth as the flaming cars came at them. At the last moment, she swerved, completing an S-shaped turn which had them weaving between the pyres.

"This is getting too bloody hairy, boss," Gray said. "You drive—"

"If you say worse than Jake you can get out," Anja snapped.

"Not what I was going to say at all."

The Agera swerved around another couple of cars then straightened.

Gray said, "The on-ramp to the freeway should be up here."

The street had straightened, and the Agera hit 120MPH and Anja pointed it at the ramp. It bellied out as it crossed the point of elevation and felt like a plane starting its climb after takeoff.

Behind the racing vehicle, the helicopter appeared again. It opened fire, and once more, asphalt erupted into the air like lava spewing from small volcanoes.

Gray looked in the side mirror and saw the rounds hitting closer. He felt his asshole pucker while waiting helplessly for the killing blow. Then came the weightlessness as the Agera launched over the top of the ramp onto the freeway.

It hit hard on landing. Anja muttered a curse as she turned the wheel, trying to catch the skid. The rear end slid out, and for a moment, the Agera thought about spinning. But Anja worked the wheel like a pro, and the rear kicked back in, and the Agera came back on track.

Anja saw the tunnels up ahead. The helicopter was closing in behind them. A glance in the mirror was enough. But the power of the Agera was supreme, and soon they were inside the glass tunnels.

However, the helicopter would not be outdone. The 12.7 mm guns opened fire, and the glass of the tunnels started to rain down like confetti. Then the helicopter fired a 70 mm rocket, bringing hell to earth.

The rocket exploded in a massive fireball. Steel joined the glass in cascading down this time. A length smashed into the rear of the Agera with brutal force. The machine wore the damage like a wound of pride.

But it wasn't done there. The orange fireball engulfed the vehicle in a warm embrace.

"Shit a brick," Gray growled.

Anja felt the heat engulf them and did the only thing possible. She went faster.

The Agera exploded from the orange cloud like a comet of raw power and speed slicing through the flames. "The bridge and river are ahead," Gray told her. "Once we get across, you need to take the exit and go south. Run along the river to the tunnels. That will stop the helicopter."

"What about them?" Anja asked.

"What?" Gray glanced in the side mirror and saw the three black SUVs. "Ah, shit."

———

"SOMETHING IS WRONG," Slania said from the back of the van Ilse was driving.

"What?" Hawk asked.

Slania looked up from the laptop. "I'm seeing reports of a helicopter firing on a vehicle that is being pursued by other vehicles.

"Anja and Gray," Hawk said.

"See if you can raise them," Ilse said.

Hawk punched in a number and let it ring. Gray never answered. "Can't get him."

"Slania, how far away are we from the incident?"

"I can direct you to intercept," Slania replied.

"Do it."

For the next few minutes, Slania was directing Ilse to the intercept position. Hawk climbed into the back and put his body armor on then loaded his 433. Once he was set, Slania did the same. Returning to the front, he held the wheel while Ilse put her armor on.

It was then that the word came from Slania. "Intercept in one mile."

"In the tunnel?"

"In the tunnel."

"Roger that."

———

THE AGERA HAD a few new holes in the rear panels, and the back window was gone. The tunnels were fast approaching. "Up there," Gray said.

Anja seemed cool and calm, except for the sheen of

sweat on her face, which told of the exertion she'd been under since the outset of the chase. The three SUVs were still back there, though without the power of the Agera. What brought the beast of a car back to the field was the uptick in traffic.

Then, of course, there was the helicopter. It was still up there and preparing for another run. Gray looked at Anja. "You know this sodding bastard will get lucky sooner or later."

"Let's hope it is later," Anja replied.

Suddenly, for some inexplicable reason, a BMW in front of them swerved the wrong way to avoid them. It went one way, and Anja swerved the other, and the Agera hit a patch of oil. For the next two hundred meters those within were just passengers as the Agera spun wildly. It disappeared inside the tunnel, hit the wall with a glancing blow and shook Anja and Gray to the core. From there it spun back into the middle of the three-lane with dizzying speed.

The rubber peeled off the rims, sending sparks flying like an angle grinder on a length of steel. Then it ground to a stop, side-on to the approaching SUVs. Anja and Gray opened their doors and pushed them up. Then they climbed out, Anja closest to the oncoming SUVs.

Pulling her P320, she opened fire at the lead vehicle. A series of holes appeared in the windscreen with each impacting round. Lines spiderwebbed across it. It wasn't until she had fired the final bullet in the magazine that the SUV suddenly veered into the concrete wall of the tunnel.

Anja then casually turned and walked around the incapacitated Agera, dropping out the empty Magazine in the P320 and reloading. Gray looked at her. "Feel better, boss?"

"Much."

The two other SUVs skidded to a halt, and their doors

were thrown open. Armed men appeared and opened fire. Anja and Gray ducked down behind the Agera as bullets began hammering into it.

Gray said, "So much for a three-million-dollar set of wheels."

"Shut up, Marcus. Start shooting."

They opened fire from behind the Agera at the shooters. The noise in the tunnel was unbelievable. Anja saw movement at the crashed SUV and saw Svetlana climb out with a weapon in her hand. "Tough bitch," the Talon boss muttered.

Using superior firepower, the shooters for the White Dove pressed forward. Gray dropped out a magazine and reloaded. The slide on Anja's P320 locked back, and she cursed. "I'm down to my last mag."

"Yeah, me too."

She glanced around, looking for a way out of their predicament. There was nothing. The tunnel had cleared behind them while the traffic was backing up at the rear of the SUVs. More bullets hammered into the Agera in the all too familiar staccato rhythm.

The two Talon operators started firing once more at the White Dove and her people. Handguns against automatic weapons. It was becoming a nonevent. Anja knew she was low, and when the slide locked back once more, it confirmed her suspicions.

She sat down with her back against the Agera. "I'm out, Marcus."

He held up his own weapon. "Me too. You got your trainers on, boss?"

Anja tucked her weapon away and said, "Ready when you are."

The roar of a motor filled the tunnel, trying to drown out the sound of the gunfire. Anja and Gray looked and saw the team van coming straight toward them on the wrong side of the road.

The van screeched to a halt, and the doors came open. The first person to appear was Hawk. He looked like a soldier's version of a fairy godmother. He walked forward and opened fire. Not with his rifle, but with the under-slung grenade launcher.

The launcher thumped, and one of the SUVs exploded. Hawk looked at Anja and Gray and said, "Don't just sit there hatching fucking eggs, get in the van."

Beside Hawk, Slania opened fire at a shooter. Ilse remained in the van with the motor running. Anja and Gray came to their feet and sprinted toward the van, and as they passed Hawk, he said, "Nice wheels, boss."

"Shut up, Jacob."

Once they had dived into the van, Hawk fired another grenade. It exploded short, but had the desired effect. He turned and ran to the van, Slania with him. They climbed in, and Hawk snapped, "Ilse, go. Get us to the plane."

The van shot forward and turned sharply. It headed at speed back the way it had come. Hawk looked at Anja and Gray. "You two okay?"

Anja nodded. Gray grinned. Hawk frowned. "What?"

"Man, the boss can fucking drive."

———

WATCHING THE VAN DRIVE AWAY, Svetlana screamed in frustration at the failure of the mission. Blood was running down her left arm, and she winced at the burning pain from the bullet crease near her shoulder.

Vadim came over to her, reloading his weapon. "Do you want us to continue?"

"What about the helicopter?" Svetlana asked.

"It is low on fuel. It can't stay in the air much longer."

The White Dove shook her head. "Let them go."

She looked at the carnage all around them. "We need to leave."

"The wounded?" Vadim asked.

"Those who can walk, we bring with us. Anyone else we leave here. But do it quickly."

Vadim knew what must be done, and it took only moments to shoot the wounded who needed urgent medical attention. With that done, their remaining personnel climbed into the drivable SUVs and left the tunnel.

Svetlana's cell buzzed. Looking down at the screen, she saw it was her father. "Yes?"

"What am I looking at, Svetlana?"

She pictured him standing in front of the large bank of screens at the castle from which he monitored world events. She said, "A small glitch, nothing more."

"I'm thinking it appears somewhat more than a small glitch, daughter. More likely a complete fuck up." There was ice in his voice. "I am growing impatient with your results, or lack thereof, Svetlana."

"This does not affect you, father. This is my business."

"Anything that affects you affects me, daughter. Especially now. Make it go away or there will be consequences."

"What do you mean consequences?" Svetlana asked.

"I will take back everything I have given you, Svetlana. I mean everything."

The line went dead. Svetlana felt an icy chill grip her heart. Not out of fear, but from the knowledge that should her father try to enact his threat, she would be forced to kill him.

CHAPTER FIFTEEN

ONCE MORE ABOARD THE MARABOU, they were headed to Berlin to collect Strike Team Falcon. From there, they would fly to Siberia. The success of the plan hinged on getting the team on site, securing the compound, and being able to use the airfield that was part of the compound. If it was suitable for the Marabou, then they had more chance of accomplishing their mission. Especially with the stealth capabilities of the Marabou.

Hawk scrolled through the intel that Slania had gathered.

Slania appeared beside him. "What do you think?" she asked.

"It all hinges on getting the Marabou down and up," Hawk replied. "The length of that runway is crucial."

"Going by satellite photos, I managed to secure, we should be able to get it down, weather permitting."

"Great. At least that is something."

Slania looked up and saw Ilse approaching. Slania said, "I'll keep working on it."

Rising to her feet, she walked away and Ilse took her

place, sitting beside Hawk and kissing him on the cheek. "It's been a while since we've been this close."

"We've been busy," he replied.

She put her head on his shoulder. "You working on an assault plan?"

"Yes."

"How is it going?"

"Slania just told me we can get the Marabou down."

"I'm guessing you're looking at inserting by parachute?"

"Yes, it would be the best way. We'll do it under the cover of darkness and work it from there."

"So, Winston, what is the plan?"

"Secure the airfield, the comms building, and the power, and take out any and all threats."

"What about the hostages?"

"We take out all threats and the hostages should be fine."

"Do you have enough bodies?" Ilse asked.

"It's not ideal, but we'll make it work."

"I'll see what I can do," Ilse said and kissed Hawk on the lips this time. "Leave it with me, babe."

Gray sat down.

Hawk sighed. "What is this, musical fucking chairs?"

"You need to up your game, Mucker," Gray said with a broad grin.

"Oh, yes?"

"Mate, the boss had that Agera doing everything but talk."

"I don't care about that," Hawk stated. "What impressed me was that she stole the bloody thing in the first place."

Gray smiled. "She looked like a pro when she did it too. How are the preliminaries coming?"

"Getting there." Hawk passed him some of the photos and other intel he was looking at.

The former para flicked through them and said, "Is the runway long enough?"

"Slania says yes."

Gray lifted his gaze. "We're a team short. We have to work on the theory they know we're coming. Another team would help no end."

"Ilse is working on it."

"I hope she can get something."

"So do I."

———

ILSE CAME THROUGH. The plane was sitting on the runway in Berlin, and two strike teams were loading up. Anja had called a meeting to fill the team leaders in on the mission details.

Falcon was led by Lex Tomlinson. A.K.A. Luthor. He was former SAS, while the rest of his team were a mix of Commandos and SBS. They were a team of four as were Strike Team Krait.

Krait was commanded by Ted Mills. He was a former commando from the 1st Commando Regiment. The rest of his people consisted of two Canadians and a Brit from the SBS.

"Glad to have you aboard, gentlemen," Anja said. "Jacob will be your field commander. Any orders on the ground will be given by him unless they are overridden. But before you become concerned about interference from command, it doesn't happen very often."

"Where are we headed, ma'am?" Tomlinson asked. "The boss only gave us instructions to meet you here."

"Siberia," Anja replied.

"Glad I didn't pack my swim trunks," Mills said. "Might have frozen my balls off. Excuse me, boss."

"What are the details?" Tomlinson asked.

"Jake will go through them with you after."

"Extract?" Mills asked.

"That depends," Hawk replied. "If you and your men can secure the airfield then we'll be good. If you can't, it'll be a long walk home."

"There might be a problem," Ilse said as she came over to them. "Weather."

"How bad?" Anja asked.

"Looks like a blizzard coming in around the time we're scheduled to drop."

"Then we drop earlier," Hawk said. "Use the conditions to our advantage."

He looked at the other commanders. Both nodded.

"That'll work," Mills said. "All the strike teams are Mountain Troop qualified."

"Same here," Tomlinson agreed.

"We'll still have the issue of getting the plane down," Anja pointed out.

"We wait it out."

"Fuel?"

"Can you have a tanker on standby?" Hawk asked.

Anja looked at Ilse. "I'll get one."

"Okay," Anja said. "We're wheels up in ten minutes. Jake will fill you in on the rest when we're up. Work out a plan and run it by me."

"Roger that," Hawk said.

———

THE PLAN WAS SIMPLE ENOUGH. Krait would secure the airfield which was a klick from the main compound. Falcon would have the power and the compound. One man, Frost, would be on overwatch. Hawk and Gray would disable the communications room and then secure the hostages.

Everything would kick off at the same time. The comms and power would be on timed charges. When they exploded, Mills would take out the tower at the airfield. On the Marabou, all outgoing transmissions would be jammed.

Now, it was time for action.

"All teams are down. Proceeding to target."

"Copy, Bravo One. Good luck."

Every operator was attired in winter gear against the biting cold. With the farthest distance to travel, Team Krait set off first.

The ferocity of the wind gusts had risen, and the flurries were coming down hard. In the darkness, the snow-covered trees stood like silent sentinels guarding the eerie landscape.

From the time they left the plane, the jump had been dicey. They had cut it fine due to the weather closing in faster than expected.

Once Krait had disappeared into the blizzard, Falcon and Bravo started on their own route through the trees.

———

40,000 Feet

With the weather closing in, the Marabou was forced to ascend quickly to get above the storms after dropping the teams. Slania was keeping track of the airfield while Ilse was watching over the teams headed to the compounds. The weather made ISR difficult but not impossible. Each team member had their personal location device activated to keep Alpha updated.

Slania looked toward Anja who was strapped into the command chair due to the air turbulence. "Krait is one klick from the airfield, boss."

"Falcon and Bravo are a similar distance from their target compound," Ilse informed her.

"Right. How are we looking on the ground?"

"Picking up various heat signatures but it is near impossible to confirm," Slania replied.

"Confirm," Ilse agreed.

Anja toggled her comm through to the cockpit. "Hammer, is there any chance we can get lower?"

"Not unless you want your fillings shook loose, ma'am," the pilot replied.

"Roger that."

"Boss, I'm getting some odd signals in my feed," Slania said.

"On the screen."

The picture changed and looked like a field of white. Slania changed the feed, and soon, an outline of the airfield came up with outbuildings, the tower, and what appeared to be vehicles. Some, however, were bigger than the others.

Anja stared at them and said, "Can you get a clearer view of those bigger vehicles?"

"I'm trying."

"Ilse, how about you?"

"Nothing."

Anja said, "See if there is any chatter to be picked up in the area. I'm getting a funny feeling about this."

Slania worked her keyboard and listened through her headphones. For a moment, there was nothing but then she picked up a faint transmission. She looked at her boss and said, "Listen to this."

Slania hooked her into the traffic. After a short moment, she said, "Let the teams know they have a problem. Possible armor on the ground. Have them decide whether to abort."

"You know they can't abort," Ilse said. "If they do they have no way out."

Anja's stare hardened. "That is for them to decide."

"Shit," Hawk growled. He toggled his comms and said, "Everyone, gather on me."

Moments later, they were all gathered around. But before Hawk started, he opened his comms and said, "Krait One, copy?"

The return transmission was garbled, but he could understand it. "I need you to listen, One. There has been a development."

"Copy, Bravo. Standing by."

"Okay, listen up. Alpha picked up traffic on the ground. It looks like they've called in reinforcements."

"What kind?" Tomlinson asked.

"Armor. Not tanks, thank fuck, but it looks like armored personnel carriers."

"What are our options?" Mills asked.

"We continue or we call it off," Hawk said.

"If we call it off, we have no way out of here," Gray pointed out.

"That is a downside."

"Well, shit," Tomlinson growled. "Looks like we go out in a blaze of fucking glory."

"Wait. Don't write us off yet," Gray said.

"What are you thinking?" Hawk asked.

"We brought extra explosives and detonators. We might be able to use that on the armor."

"Alpha Two, copy?"

"Copy, Bravo," Ilse replied.

"What is the tally on the armor?"

"Five. Two at the airfield, three at the compound. Unknown hostiles."

"Roger. Standby." Hawk spoke briefly to Mills. "Krait One, you have two armored vehicles on target."

"Roger, Bravo. We'll handle it. Even if I have to piss in the gas tank."

"Roger that." Hawk now turned his attention to Tomlinson. "Three on-site."

"We'll need to place the charges before we do anything else."

"Yes."

"I need one full charge," Gray said. "I'll place it on the barracks."

"We still need enough for the power and comms hut," Hawk pointed out.

"We can divide it. Just one block should be enough."

"Are we sure about this?" Hawk asked.

"It's not like we have another option," Tomlinson said.

"All right then. Alpha, we're Charlie Mike."

"Roger, Bravo. You are continuing your mission. Good luck."

Krait made their way through the snowstorm with surprisingly good speed. Reaching the airfield, they split into two teams. Mills and Buttons, Kramer and Stripes. Mills said to Kramer, "I need you to secure the tower. Once it's clear, place your charges but don't detonate."

"Roger that."

"Take down any guards you come across. No one extra should be out on a shit night like tonight."

"Except the unintelligent like us."

"Isn't that the truth."

They moved silently through the storm across the open ground in their snow camouflage. Mills and Buttons came upon a BTR-80. It was an armored personnel carrier. Mills stood guard while Buttons placed the charge.

As luck would have it, the second of the armored vehi-cles, the same model, was parked close by. With the second charge placed, the two men from Strike Team Krait, moved on.

"I've got a guard on the east side near the tower," Kramer said over his comms to Stripes. "Hold position."

Kramer pulled his suppressed Glock and moved forward through the swirling snow. His NVGs revealing the path he needed to take to get close to the guard. Once he was within safe range, the Glock came up, and he put a bullet into the man's head.

"X-ray down," he said softly into his comms.

Stripes joined Kramer, and the two set about laying charges at the base of the tower. A few minutes later, the explosive device was right to go.

Meanwhile, Mills and Buttons had moved along to a Mil Mi-24 helicopter. Mills placed another charge on it and then they retreated into the snowstorm to rendezvous with the rest of their team.

Once they were dug in, Mills toggled his comms. "Krait One to all callsigns. We're all green and waiting for instructions."

"Krait One, from Bravo. Standby."

"Roger that. Krait One standing by."

———

FALCON EMERGED from the storm on target and planted their charges on the three armored vehicles before moving on to the power and the barracks. The barracks were on the west side of the compound. Frost and Marlborough took that task. They came in unseen by the guard and planted the charge beneath the building.

Tomlinson and Peters circled around to the power source. The original plan was to have a sniper out, but the storm had killed that idea.

The compound was reliant on a large generator for its power with an equally large backup generator just in case.

Tomlinson took up a watch position while Peters set the charges on both. Once they were detonated, the power would be cut to the compound and airfield.

So, with the power, the barracks, and the armor done, Falcon now waited on Hawk and Gray to complete their portion of the mission.

CHAPTER SIXTEEN

HAWK AND GRAY paused momentarily to check for hostiles before walking across the open area toward the communications building. The snow had abated somewhat. Using hand signals, Hawk indicated to the hut. The pair moved swiftly across the clearing until they reached the door. Gray tried the handle and found it unlocked.

Hawk nodded as Gray eased it open, and the former SAS operator slipped through the opening.

There were two men inside, both with their backs to the door. However, they must have sensed the shift in temperature because both looked around at the same time.

The suppressed 433 in Hawk's hand spat death, and both men died almost silently.

Leaving the bodies where they fell, the two operators moved quickly to complete their tasks. Hawk placed a small charge and set it to detonate. "All right, Mucker, let's get this party started."

Moving back outside, they took cover behind a large storage pile of supplies. Then Hawk said into his comms, "All callsigns standby."

"Roger, standing by."

"Standing by."

"On my mark. Three...two...one...execute."

And things went boom.

The execution was perfect. Everyone was trained to perfection, and this was what they could do. When the barracks went up, a large hole was immediately punched into the forces of the White Dove. The tower came down, and the power went out, cutting all lines of communication.

The attackers moved in and methodically began taking control of their objectives. Like wraiths, several figures emerged from the falling snow and darkness. All were dispatched before they could gather themselves. Even though they were prepared, the Talon operation was that much better.

A larger group materialized out of night, backlit by the burning buildings. Hawk pulled a grenade and removed the pin. Launching it to fall among the confused group, it detonated almost immediately, and they fell apart like ten pins.

For the next twenty minutes, the teams worked tirelessly until they had control of both areas. Then Hawk made the call. "Alpha, you are cleared for landing."

"Roger, see you soon. Good work, team."

———

IT WAS Tomlinson who located the girls. They were being kept in a building on the west side of the compound. Once he'd found them, he called it in. "Bravo One, west side. I've got the packages."

"Roger, Falcon One. What number?"

"Seven."

"I'll be right there."

Hawk and Gray made their way over to the building

through the storm. The inside was lit by the strike Team's flashlights. The seven women were young, perhaps late teens at a stretch. They were dirty and cold and frightened.

"Where are they from?" Hawk asked.

"Germany, Lithuania, Romania, France," Tomlinson replied.

"Who here speaks the best English?" Hawk asked.

"I do," said a young woman with black hair stepping forward. "I did university in England."

Hawk turned to Gray. "Take one of the Falcon guys and find us some wheels."

"Roger that."

"How long have you all been here?"

"A week, maybe more. Some of us have been here longer."

"Where were you meant to go?"

"We heard mention of a castle somewhere in the Urals," the girl replied.

"A castle? Are you sure?"

"Yes—no. It's what was heard."

"Do you know where in the Urals?"

"No." She looked at him questioningly. "Are you really going to take us home?"

"Yes, lass, you'll be going home."

In the cone of the flashlight, he saw her eyes well with tears. Hawk turned away and said, "Alpha, copy?"

"Copy, Bravo."

"We have secured seven, I repeat, seven packages. Moving to extract."

"Roger, Bravo. See you when we get there."

Hawk glanced at Tomlinson. "Get them ready to move, Lex. The sooner we're out of this cold hole, the better."

"LET'S get some flares on the runway," Mills barked through the storm's noise. "That bird is almost here."

Two of his team commandeered a truck and took it along the runway. One drove while the second threw flares along the perimeter. At the end they turned and repeated the procedure. With the task complete, Hawk called the Marabou. "Hammer One-One, this is Krait One, copy?"

"Copy, Krait One. Send traffic."

"Hammer, runway is lit, crosswinds are easing, visibility poor. Good luck, over."

"Roger that. Hammer inbound."

Ten minutes later, Mills and his team were still waiting when eventually they heard the roar of massive turbofans coming out of the storm. Then, like a giant lumbering bird of prey, the Marabou appeared.

"Fuck!" Mills exclaimed. "Hammer, pull up! Pull up! You're on the wrong side of the flares."

The sound from the plane grew instantly louder as the pilots engaged full thrust. The Marabou seemed to moan out loud as it clawed its way back into the air, the giant wheels barely inches above the snow.

Mills and his men held their collective breaths, willing the plane not to crash into the soft snow and mud beside the runway. The team leader could picture the pilots trying to manually lift the beast back into the air.

Then, with a swirl of snow and grit kicked up by the turbofans, the Marabou disappeared, the only sign of its passing the roar of the engines.

"Fuck me," Mills growled. "Hammer One-One, what the fuck was that?"

"Let's call it a near miss," the pilot called back. "We're going around."

The second attempt was a lot better. The Marabou touched down and taxied to the apron, where the rear ramp came down. Anja and Ilse appeared at the head of the ramp to greet the team leader. Mills looked at Anja and said, "You lot like living dangerously?"

"I have no idea what you mean. Where are the others?"

"Not here yet."

"How far away?"

"Bravo, copy?" Mills said into his comms.

"Copy, Krait One."

"ETA? Your boss is getting impatient."

"Two mikes. We're coming in with a borrowed ride. Don't shoot us."

"They'll be right along, ma'am," Mills said to Anja.

As if on cue, the truck came rumbling out of the storm with a deep-throated roar. It pulled over near the plane and Tomlinson's men began to help the young women alight. Hawk hurried up the ramp.

"Wonders will never cease, Mr. Hawk," Anja said. "You are still alive."

Hawk winked. "Only the good die young, boss. Me, I'll live forever."

Ilse smiled, relieved that her man was safe.

"Get everyone aboard," Anja said simply. "Let's get out of here."

———

THE MAN who'd brought the news to Svetlana was lying dead on the flagstone floor, his life blood pooling and drying quickly around him. Her anger at being thwarted once more had become too much, boiling over as she responded with a furious inferno.

Vadim looked down at the dead man and then at his boss. "He did not deserve that, Svetlana."

Only he could get away with speaking to her like that. Instead of lashing out at him, she nodded. "You are right. He did not. But it is too late now."

The only glimmer of hope in the whole debacle was the fact that the girls set for the banquet the following evening had already arrived at the castle.

Before his untimely demise, the dead messenger had informed them of how contact had been lost with the compound. When a small recon force had been sent to investigate, they had found all of the men there dead, and the compound virtually destroyed. Worse still, the girls were gone.

"How did they know?" Svetlana asked. "How?"

Vadim stared at her. "Declan Hunter."

"Of course, it was him. Damn it. I want security doubled for tomorrow night."

"Do you think that they would be crazy enough to come here?" Vadim asked.

"Expect the unexpected, Vadim. Expect the unexpected."

"I will see to it."

"Can you be a sweetie and get rid of the body?"

"Yes, ma'am."

"Then come back tonight. I need something to relax me."

———

THE SATELLITE PICTURES told the story. "It is the only castle in the Urals," Slania said. "It has to be it."

"Right, get us in there," Hawk said.

The team was in Finland refueling and rearming.

Ilse frowned at him. "What is your plan, Jake?"

"Simple. Get in, kill the old prick and then get out."

Anja shook her head. "No. The mission is done. We handed the girls over to Interpol, we shut down the compound where Svetlana holds her prisoners, and now we have to wait until she comes out of Russia. Once she does, we pick her up then."

"Come on, boss, let us have a sneak and peek at least."

"I have to worry about getting you out, Jake," Anja pointed out. "It is miles from nowhere. It has come to my attention that just recently I can't trust my contacts."

"I know someone."

Anja rolled her eyes. "Of course you would."

"He can get me and Marcus out," Hawk assured her. "No problem."

"If I agree to this, Jake, it is an intelligence mission only. You look, take pictures, and get out. Anything to do with trafficking. Anything with the coup, ignore."

"Cross my heart."

"Shit. One more thing, you'll jump in daylight. I'm not going to have you get hurt jumping in the dark."

"We've got this, boss."

Anja looked at Gray. "Marcus?"

"I go where Jake goes, boss."

"Don't make me regret this."

———

ILSE GAVE Hawk a beer and sat down beside him. She said, "Do you have all the equipment you need?"

Hawk wiped his mouth with the back of his hand. "Yes. We should be good."

"You're not going to do anything stupid, are you?"

"I promise to be on my best behavior," Hawk replied.

"I'm serious, Jake. There is no backup and you're miles from anywhere."

"We'll be fine."

"Who is this friend you were talking about?" Ilse asked.

"His name is Pavel. Former Russian Special Forces but now runs a gulag."

"Russia doesn't have gulags anymore," Ilse replied.

"That's what they want you to think."

"But then why would he help you?"

Hawk grinned. "Because I saved his life once in Syria. ISIS had captured him. He was being held in a camp my SAS team infiltrated looking for a British captive. We found them both in the same cell. Couldn't leave him behind so we took him with us."

"And now you are good friends?"

"I wouldn't exactly say that. Not good friends..."

———

"NOT ANY TYPE of fucking friends if you ask me," Gray growled, staring at the six men before them pointing their AKs at them.

"It's been a while," Hawk replied.

Hawk had reached out to Pavel, who assured him that he could get him to the castle and out again when required. He said he would send some men to meet them.

The men who stood before the pair right then looked at them with murder in their eyes.

"Are you sure that these are the people we're meant to meet?" Gray asked.

Hawk stared at them. The men were dressed in old, warm clothing and were unshaven. Hawk said, "Who the fuck else would they be?"

"Deserters?"

"What?"

Gray said, "I heard that there were deserters who hung out in the Urals."

"Who told you that load of bollocks?"

"Some bloody sergeant-major in the paras. Can't remember his name."

One of the Russians stepped forward. He said, "Who are you?"

"We are here to meet Pavel," Hawk replied.

Suddenly, the Russians grew angry and started to shuffle forward. The leader held up his hand. "Are you friends of his?"

"Ah shit," Gray said in realization. "This lot are escapees from the fucking gulag."

The leader smiled. Through his beard, Hawk could see into his open mouth. There were black gaps between yellow teeth. Hawk said, "Mate, you need to get your money back from your dentist."

The man glared at Hawk. His face contorted into a snarl, and the AK came up to fire. Then suddenly, gunshots ripped through the air, and each of the six escaped prisoners from the gulag spasmed before falling into the snow.

"Holy crap," growled Gray. "What the fuck was that?"

A handful of men emerged from the snow-covered trees beside them. Immediately, Hawk recognized the leader. "Hello, Pavel."

"Jacob, my friend. How are you doing this fine day?"

"A lot fucking better than what I would have been doing in 5 minutes time, I can tell you now."

"Yes, I forgot to tell you, the forest and the mountains are full of the escapees from the gulags."

"You could have remembered."

"Not to worry, I am here now. Tell me, what is this all about?"

Hawk and Gray bent down and picked up their

suppressed 433s. "We are on a sneak and peek mission, my friend."

"Really? Tell me about it."

"Have you ever heard of the Silver Fox?" Hawk asked.

Pavel nodded. "I have heard of him. They say he's a bad man. His daughter is worse. How you would say *easy on the eye, hard on the dick.*"

"I've seen what she can do," Hawk informed him. "The bitch is batshit crazy."

"So what interests you?"

"It looks like Boris is organizing backers for a tilt at the presidency."

Pavel's eyebrows shot up. "Are you saying he is getting backers for a coup?"

"Yes, we stumbled across it by mistake. Our real target is his daughter, Svetlana."

"Why her?" Pavel asked.

She was working with some mercenaries, paying them to kidnap women off the street or in other countries so she could buy them and then use them for whatever means."

"What do you need me to do?"

Hawk said, "Can you guide us to his castle?"

"I cannot, but one of my men can."

"We will be there for a day or two," Hawk said. "After that, we need a way out of the country."

Pavel nodded. "Anything for my friend, Jacob."

"Thanks, Pavel."

The Russian turned to his men. He motioned one of them forward. "Igor will guide you."

"Do you trust him?" Hawk asked.

"I would trust him more than I trust you, my British friend." Pavel smiled. "And that is not very much."

"Fuck you too."

"Come, I have a surprise for you."

Hawk and Gray followed him back into the trees

along with his men. After walking for a short distance, they came across a handful of snowmobiles. "You will take three. Igor will need one to get back."

"Thank you, my friend," Hawk said. "I will see you in a couple of days."

"Do not bring any trouble with you, Jacob."

"I will try not to."

The trio traveled for four hours to reach the valley. Stopping within a line of trees, they looked out over the steep sides. On the far side stood a castle on a cliff face. The walls were made of rock, with great gray slab sides.

"I guess that is it," Hawk said.

Gray pointed to the left. "I guess if we move up the mountain a bit farther, we might be able to see inside."

"We'll have to leave the snowmobiles here," Hawk agreed.

"All right then, let's do it."

Hawk and Gray packed up what they needed and began the arduous climb higher up the mountain. An hour later, they found a place that was sheltered but provided a good vantage point over the castle. "This will do."

Hunkering down for the night, Hawk called in on the sat phone they had with them. Ilse picked up on the other end. "We're all good. On target and settling in for the night."

"What is the weather like?" Ilse asked.

"It's cold, but it doesn't look like there's a storm coming in."

"That's good."

"Remember those snow-covered postcards of the castles that you get?"

"Yes."

"It kind of looks like that."

"It must be nice, then," Ilse said.

"No, it's shit. I hate those fluffy bloody things," Hawk told Ilse.

"I bet you were the Christmas grinch."

"We didn't have Christmas," Hawk replied.

"Go on with you. I'll be waiting for your next check-in."

The serenity of the valley was suddenly shattered by a low-flying transport helicopter. It circled over the castle before dropping down into the courtyard.

Hawk brought up his binoculars. Gray had only just gone to sleep before his turn for watch, when it rocked him awake. "What the fuck is going on, Jake?"

"Looks like Boris has got visitors," Hawk replied.

Gray grabbed his binoculars, and they watched as the helicopter's rotor wound down. Passengers appeared as they walked across the courtyard. Hawk grabbed a camera with a telephoto zoom lens. "I hope this is long enough."

As he began taking pictures, he said to Gray, "Get on the SAT phone and call Alpha. Tell her we've got some pictures coming her way."

"Roger that."

In all, there were eight couples brought in by the helicopter. Minutes after they had alighted, the rotors spun back up and the helicopter lifted into the sky. It was only moments later when the second one appeared.

"Do you think this is the function we've been hearing about?" Gray asked.

"Could be," Hawk replied.

An additional eight couples got off the second helicopter and were escorted inside. Then, like the previous one, having disgorged its load, the rotors spun back up, and it lifted into the sky, flying along the valley.

Hawk said, "What I'd give to be a fly on the wall inside that place."

"Well, they're down there. We're up here."

"We could always go for a squint," Hawk said.

"No, Jake. You know what the boss said."

"Have you got that drone in your kit?"

"Yes."

"Get it out, Marcus, we'll send it over for a look."

Gray grabbed his pack and removed the drone. It was an Indago 4, manufactured by Lockheed Martin. Weighing in at just over 4.5 pounds, it had a range of 8 miles, which put it well within the operational parameters of the current mission.

Then there was the high-resolution camera system which allowed the operator to identify what they were looking at, either day or night.

Once the drone was ready, Gray tested it before launching it. It flew out over the abyss and on toward the castle. According to the drone, the distance it covered across the valley was two miles.

Gray brought it to a hover over the castle where the camera could rove the structure. They picked up the guards. All were armed with AK-12s and dressed in heavy winter clothing. They counted six guards outside.

After another circuit, they discovered that apart from a helicopter, there was only one other way in. That was by cable car. "Talk about Where Eagles fucking Dare," Hawk growled.

"What?" Gray asked.

"You not seen the movie? Clint Eastwood, Richard Burton?"

"No idea what you're talking about."

Hawk was aghast. "It's a bloody classic, mate."

"If you say so. Look, what do we have here?"

The screen was showing a large dome constructed of reinforced glass. Gray readjusted the camera and zoomed in. It was like magic. The picture grew as it focused on what was beneath the dome. What they were looking at was a large room. There were two people. Hawk frowned. "Is that..."

Gray nodded. "Everyone's favorite bird."

"Oh, mate," Hawk said. "This is fucking gold."

———

EVERY DIGNITARY EXTENDED an invitation had accepted and were present. The generals, Maksim Gabulov and Viktor Bobyor, and Admiral Aleksey Golovin. Also, there was Elmir Kuzmin, and Yury Smolov, two powerful politicians at the Kremlin.

It was Admiral Golovin who approached Svetlana soon after his arrival. Although married, his wife had remained home due to her advancing pregnancy. "I was told you would have entertainment, Svetlana. I do hope you might be part of it."

She was wearing a white dress with a plunging neckline and cut even lower at the back. Svetlana's smile was filled with ice as she said, "Is the orchestra not enough for you, Admiral?"

"If I wanted to listen to music, I would have stayed at home."

"What is your taste?"

"I'm feeling a little Far East, almost Scandinavian even."

Svetlana took his hand. "Come with me."

"That would be nice," he replied.

Ignoring the comment, Svetlana took him to another wing of the castle. He was escorted into a large room with a king-sized bed and all the luxury trimmings.

"Wait here," Svetlana said.

The admiral nodded and watched lasciviously as Svetlana started to walk away then stopped. When she turned back to him, she had a suppressed handgun in her hand.

Golovin was still trying to work out where it had been hidden when she shot him in the head.

————

"WHAT WAS THAT ALL ABOUT?" Hawk asked as he watched the shooting unfold on the screen. "I thought this was about drumming up support, not killing it. How much longer can that drone stay on station?"

"We've got spare powerpacks. We can use it all night if we need to."

"Keep it over the castle for the time being. Something isn't right."

CHAPTER SEVENTEEN

WHEN SVETLANA RETURNED to the gathering, she found her father talking to a couple of politicians who were new to the Kremlin. Orlov raised his eyebrows and said, "There you are, my dear. Where have you been?"

"Attending to business, father."

"This is Kirill and Ivan. This is my daughter Svetlana. If you would go with her, she will make sure you enjoy yourself."

Svetlana smiled. "It would be my pleasure, gentlemen."

The two middle-aged men followed her closely, staring at her rear as she walked with unwavering concentration. She took these men to a different room. This time, when she told them to wait, she actually left the room.

On her return a short time later, Svetlana was in the company of two young ladies from Romania. These were experienced girls, not the new ones which would be intimidated and scared.

"I trust you gentlemen will be happy with the evening's entertainment?"

"I do think so, Svetlana," Ivan answered, eyeing the

girls before choosing the one he wanted. "I do think so, indeed."

She left them in the capable hands of the young women. From there, she went to find Vadim. "Have you taken care of the other matter?"

"Yes."

"Good. Keep an eye on the other guests. Let me know if there are issues."

"I will."

Svetlana went back to the main hall. Her father was mingling among the guests, testing the waters before taking things further. "Are my new friends being taken care of?"

"Yes, father. I have two of my most experienced girls with them."

"Good, good. Now, I must talk to my generals. We will be in my library."

"Would you like me to join you?"

"No, no. See to the guests."

"Yes, father."

———

"WOULD you like another glass of vodka, gentlemen?" Orlov asked Bobyor and Gabulov.

Both generals nodded. Gabulov said, "Nothing lubricates the bitterness of business better than vodka."

Orlov poured the drinks and then went and stood beside the blazing open fire. He sipped his drink and stared at the two men before him. "I will talk to the others eventually, but it is you I wanted to address first. Because without your help, I cannot do this."

"Do what?" Bobyor asked.

"Remove President Smolnikov from power." Orlov let the words sink in before he continued. "The President is growing weak. He is making promises to the west to reduce our nuclear arsenal and to cut the size of our armed forces. It will leave us weak in the eyes of NATO at a time when we must show strength."

"How do you propose to do this?" Gabulov asked.

"Why do you think everyone is here?"

"Golovin won't stand for it," Babyor pointed out.

"He has been taken care of."

Gabulov nodded. "Tell us everything."

AN HOUR LATER, all vestiges of daylight had faded. The night sky was clear of cloud, and a big silver room moon hung over the Ural Mountains. It turned the landscape pale, and the snow took on a bright, glistening silver effect. The valley was quiet, silent almost. Except for the low hum of the drone.

With the observation mission going smoothly and according to plan, Hawk had a feeling that their luck couldn't last. When things are going too well, there was always a fly in the ointment. Their fly was the arrival of a patrol.

Needing a stretch, Hawk rolled onto his back and sat up, glancing around as he drank some water from his canteen. In the moonlight behind them he noticed a patrol filing through the trees. He reached for his 433 and said, "We've got visitors."

"Shit," Gray muttered. "Give me a moment."

"What are you doing?"

"I need to set this thing down to help you."

"You sure?"

"Yeah."

Hawk turned his attention back to the patrol. There were six of them. All armed and dressed for the cold. "I'm ready," Gray said.

"You hook around to the right. When you're in position, let me know."

Moving silently back down the slope through the rocks, Hawk climbed again and positioned himself above their camp. Gray had now managed to get around the flank of the patrol. Things appeared to be on their side.

"Two is in position."

"Hold," Hawk replied.

Hawk knew the patrol would discover the camp. But he wanted them distracted when they opened fire. He watched them closing the distance to the camp until the point man discovered it.

"Now."

Both men opened fire with their 433s. The patrol was hammered hard. Bullets cut down the men before they even realized what was happening. They even had no time to fire back.

Hawk and Gray rose and closed in, finishing off the remaining members as they went. By the time they reached their camp, all six patrol men were dead. Gray said, "That's torn it. Time to leave."

"I want to get into that castle," Hawk said.

"Are you shitting me?" Gray was aghast. "It won't be long and this place will be swarming with cocks looking for this bloody patrol."

"Which means, old son, they'll be looking outward and not in."

"The boss won't go for it."

"Have you ever heard of the saying about asking for forgiveness rather than permission?"

"Ah shit, we're going to die."

"Have a bit of faith, Mucker. These Russians aren't that smart."

"It wasn't them I was talking about."

"Grab the gear that you need and leave the rest," Hawk said. "This will be fun."

"How are we going to get in?"

"That is the best bit."

———

"THIS IS A FUCKING STUPID IDEA," Gray growled. "We're just going to ride the cable car up to the top and get off?"

It had taken them an hour to get into position to infiltrate the castle. In that time, they had deliberately missed a check in. Hawk had also turned off the sat phone.

"Where is your sense of adventure?"

"What about the security cameras?"

"Use your gadget."

Hawk was talking about a small black box that would block the feed from the cable car. "Now, let's go."

There was only one guard on duty at the cable car house. Hawk shot him from cover before they emerged. Gray flicked on his magic transmitter, and the feed from the house disappeared at the other end. The same thing happened when they climbed onto the cable car itself.

Once they were clear of the house, the feed would come back up, and the security guard at the top would assume that it was a glitch. Hopefully.

That was the plan.

And, of course, all carefully laid plans succeeded, right?

Which was why when they reached the top, Svetlana was waiting for them with an armed detail.

Gray looked over at Hawk. "You're a fucking pillock."

———

"THERE IS A PROBLEM," Vadim told Svetlana. "Contact has been lost with one of the patrols and the cameras at the cable car have been glitching."

"They are here," she whispered to him.

"That would be my guess."

"This will be a great opportunity to find out what they know."

"Yes, ma'am."

"You have a team ready?" she asked.

"Yes."

"Then let us go out to greet them."

———

"YOU DIDN'T HAVE to dress up just to meet me," Hawk told Svetlana. "I mean, you must be cold."

Gray nodded. "She is definitely cold. Bits don't stick out like that when you're burning hot."

"I don't know, Mucker, I've seen bits like that stick out when—"

"If you are quite finished," Svetlana growled.

They nodded. "Okay, we're finished."

"Lock them away. I'll deal with them later."

Gray raised his hand.

"What?"

"Can I be kept separate from this dick? I'm not talking to him—"

Vadim stepped forward and hit the former para in the stomach. Gray doubled over in a coughing fit. He straightened up and said, "I guess that is a no."

The pair was escorted down a steep stone stairway to a creepy old dungeon. The cell was constructed totally of stone except for the door which was wood with iron straps and a barred window. "At least we have lights," Hawk said after they were locked in.

"You're a bloody knob," Gray shot back at him.

"What did I do?"

"I want to have a look in the castle...blah, blah, blah."

"You didn't have to come."

"How about you come up with a way we can get out of here," Gray said.

"I'm working on it."

An hour later, the door to the cell opened. Vadim appeared and looked at Hawk. "You come with me."

"I'd rather not."

Vadim stepped forward. "Now."

"All right, all right." He turned to Gray. "If I don't come back, I'll leave my dog to you."

"You don't have a fucking dog."

"Yeah, right."

Vadim and the men with him escorted Hawk back up the stairs to the ground floor. From there, they traversed a long hallway to a large room adorned with wall-to-wall bookcases and a large fire. Leather chairs were spread out around a solid desk.

Pushed into a chair, Hawk was secured to it with zippy ties. Then he waited a short while before the door opened, and two people entered the room: Svetlana and her father.

The Silver Fox stared at Hawk. "So, you are one of the mercenaries who are causing me no end of trouble."

Hawk shrugged. "It started out as you but in fact it was your lovely offspring that turned out to be the real target."

"What do you mean?"

Hawk saw no real issue with telling them. "We target people traffickers. Mostly to do with the sex trade. You don't really interest us. Svetlana, on the other hand, just happens to be our bread and butter."

"You are Talon?"

"That's right."

"You took down Medusa?"

"You, sir, are on a roll."

"What do your people know about what I am doing?" Orlov asked.

"You mean the whole coup thing? Not much."

"We should kill him now, father," Svetlana said.

Orlov ignored his daughter. "What about my daughter?"

Hawk said, "Put it this way, the world now knows the face of the White Dove and the Silver Fox. Especially Interpol."

"What happened to Declan Hunter?" Svetlana asked.

"Interpol has him. He was singing up a storm the last I heard." Hawk stared at Svetlana. "Who was the poor sod you shot earlier?"

Her eyes flashed in alarm. She glanced at her father, whose curiosity was now piqued by Hawk's comment.

The former SAS man grinned. "Oops. Did I let the cat out of the bag?"

"What is he talking about?" Orlov asked.

"The sod she shot," Hawk replied. "About the same distance as what we are now."

Orlov finally worked out what Hawk was talking about. "You shot Aleksey?"

There was no denying it. "Yes."

"But why? I told you to look after him, not kill him. Now I have to find another to bring the navy onto my side."

Svetlana shook her head. "I'm sorry, Papa, but what you are doing is wrong."

"Wrong? Wrong?" The pitch of his voice rose an octave. "I am trying to bring our country back to the old ways. Who are you to tell me that it is wrong? You, a human trafficker. Now you have set everything back months. You knew how important this was to me."

"Maybe in that time you will reconsider," Svetlana said.

There was bitterness in Orlov's expression. "If your brother was here—"

"But he isn't, is he, old man. He abandoned us long ago."

"He did not abandon us, you silly girl. He went to make his own way, just as I had to."

"Oh yes, the Pale Crow, how fucking original." The derision was there for the world to see.

"If you two want some privacy, I could leave," Hawk said.

"Shut up," Svetlana hissed. She turned her gaze back onto her father. "Maybe it is time I made my own way. I hate this fucking freezing place. It is colder than a witch's tit."

"Fine, go," Orlov said. "But if you ever interfere with my business again, I will kill you."

It might have been said in the heat of battle, or the Silver Fox may have meant it, but at that moment, everything blew up spectacularly. Svetlana's handgun appeared just as it had done when she had killed Golovin.

The weapon pointed at her father's head, and she pulled the trigger. His head snapped back, and the man known as the Silver Fox collapsed into a heap on the floor. His daughter spat at him and said, "You will never speak to me like that ever again."

"Well, that's that," Hawk muttered.

"Take him back to the cell," Svetlana ordered. "Vadim, the party is over. Set the charges."

"Whoa," said Hawk. "What charges?"

"My father always knew that the castle would be

212

breached one day and had demolition charges laid throughout in preparation. Now is the time to use them."

"What about all the people that are here? The girls?" Vadim asked.

Svetlana screwed up her face in disdain. "Traitors all. The only decent people are my own. The girls can be replaced."

Hawk said, "Man, I'd hate to live in your circle."

"Get him out of here," Svetlana snarled. "I'm sorry I won't be here to see you die, Mr. Hawk."

"You could always stay and we could face the bright light together holding hands," Hawk said with a grin.

"Fuck black humor."

"It's a lifestyle choice. Be seeing you, Svetlana. Ivan."

"It is Vadim," Vadim said.

The grin came back to Hawk. "No, mate, your name is whatever I want to fucking call you."

Vadim pointed at the two other guards in the room. "You, you, get him back to the cells and then find me."

Untying Hawk, they began escorting him back to the cells, traveling along a deserted hallway to the head of the stairs before starting down. One man in front, the other behind. They were about halfway down when Hawk made his move.

He flicked his foot out like a striking snake so that it hooked around the ankle of the man in front of him. The guard tripped, lost his balance and tumbled forward.

The sight of his comrade falling down the stairs gave the guard behind Hawk reason to pause. Taking advantage, Hawk spun around and rammed a fist into the man's crotch.

The impact elicited an immediate groan, and the man buckled at the knees, nausea sweeping through him. With the guard's position lower, Hawk drove a fist into his throat, smashing his larynx. The man gagged.

With some swift movements, Hawk managed to stand over him and break his neck with a savage twist.

Bending low, the former SAS man picked up the fallen guard's AK-12 and started down the stairs toward the remaining Russian.

The guard had sustained a broken leg in the fall. It was twisted at an awkward angle, but the man was stunned from smashing his head against the solid stone wall, and the pain hadn't filtered through just yet.

Without being aware that Hawk was there, the Talon operator brought the AK savagely down and knocked him out cold.

He checked the man's pockets and muttered a curse. No keys to the cell. Hawk turned and climbed back to the other man, searched him and found what he needed. Hawk grabbed the second AK and started back down the stairs.

The key rattled in the lock when Hawk inserted it. He was forced to use some strength when he gave it a twist. Inside the mechanism, there was a clunk, and the door opened.

Gray stared at him then at the weapons he was holding. "Who'd you kill to get them?"

"I'll tell you later. But for now, we need to move. This place is going to blow."

Gray took the AK. "Seriously?"

"As a bullet in the head."

Gray followed Hawk to the stairs. "Who would want to do that?"

"The girl, right after she shot her father."

"Why?"

"Family squabble. Now, enough questions, let's move."

They climbed the stairs and found their way out

without any trouble. The night air was icy, funneling down the valley before hitting the wall and climbing.

Keeping to the shadows, Hawk and Gray made their way to the cable car only to find it was under guard when they reached it. As was the helipad.

Gray said, "Looks like they're going to use that to get out."

Hawk stopped. "Bloody hell."

"What?" Gray was confused.

"We can't leave."

"Why not?"

"Because of the ones we'll be leaving to die."

"What do you mean?"

"We have to get the girls out."

"We don't know how long we have, Jake," Gray pointed out.

"We can't leave them, Marcus. I don't give a shit about the others. But those girls never asked for this."

"Shit. Ilse is going to be pissed with you if you die."

"I won't be around to worry about it now, will I?"

"Fuck."

They turned and headed back to the castle.

CHAPTER EIGHTEEN

THERE WAS ONLY one way to do it. Fast and loud. What came next was reminiscent of a scene from a John Wick movie. The first to die was the guard at the main door. He saw them coming, raised his hand, barked an order, and died when Hawk shot him, blowing his brains across the hardwood door behind him.

Gray shouldered the door open, and they walked into a large reception area. There was a handful of men and women standing there smoking and chatting.

They took one look at the armed men, and their relaxed joviality turned to concern. That went a step further when Gray shot the guard against the wall. Cries of alarm and fear echoed through the chamber.

"Get out!" Hawk snarled at them. "Get out now before the whole place blows."

They milled around like confused sheep. Wanting to flee but their brains not functioning at the correct speed. Hawk fired the AK to get them moving. It did not have the desired effect. "Fuck it."

Entering a long hallway, they began to run, Hawk pointing at a door about halfway along. "Check in there."

Gray opened it but found the room empty. "Clear."

Hawk checked the next one along. "Clear. This will take all bloody night. We need help."

An armed man appeared ahead of them. Hawk and Gray pointed their weapons at him and started barking orders.

"Put it down! Put it down!"

The man dropped his gun. His hands were raised. Hawk said, "You need to get everyone out. Do you understand the place is going to blow up?"

Alarm registered on the man's face. Suddenly he wasn't an enemy, just another human trying to get out alive. He turned and ran, shouting.

———

SUDDENLY, the courtyard where the helipad sat was filling up. Others were headed toward the cable car. Svetlana was confused. "What is happening?"

Vadim came over to her. "They know about the charges."

"How?"

"I do not know."

"Where is the helicopter?"

"A couple of minutes."

Viktor Bobyor appeared. "Svetlana, what is happening? Where is your father?"

"I don't know where he is," Svetlana lied.

"What is it I hear about a bomb?"

"Terrorists," Svetlana said. "Go to the cable car. We must get everyone away."

The Russian general nodded. "Yes."

Suddenly, the sound of a helicopter rotor came from out of the darkness. Svetlana wasn't the only one to hear it because many began hurrying toward the helipad. "Damn. Hold them back."

"How?"

"Shoot them if you have to."

Vadim signaled to his men. "Drive them back. No one gets on the helicopter."

———

THEY HAD TEN GIRLS. Three were in a drugged stupor while the rest seemed calm. They were probably drugged as well, just enough to take the edge off. In finding them, they had also killed four of the Fox's bodyguards.

Now they were coming back out, and the first thing they heard was the sound of gunfire punctuating the beat of helicopter blades. Opening the door to exit, they were greeted by floodlit chaos.

There were bodies on the ground lying in the snow, no longer pristine, but red and pink from blood stains. The helicopter was on the pad and being loaded with passengers. More gunfire, and Hawk saw someone in a suit buckle at the knees and fall face down. "Come on, let's get to our only other option. There can't be much time left if they're leaving now."

They herded the girls toward the cable cars. There was a crowd there as well. And the cars weren't moving. "This is useless, Jake," Gray said.

Hawk looked around, then back at the cable car. "Fuck it. We weren't meant to live forever."

"Jake, what are you doing?"

"Get them on the cable car."

"It's going nowhere."

"It will be. Just get them on."

They forced their way through the crowd of people. A

man blocked Gray's passage. The former para swung the AK in his grasp and dropped the man where he stood. They kept pressing forward until they reached the cable car house and forced their way in.

"Get them onboard," Hawk shouted at Gray.

The former para ushered them on, along with some others who got lost in the mix. He saw Hawk climbing the outside. "What are you doing?"

"The only thing stopping this from moving is the emergency brakes. Disable them, and we're home free."

"Be fucked, you'll kill us all."

"We're dead anyway. This way, we might have a chance."

"I bloody hate you, Jake. Just thought you should know."

"Strap yourself in."

Gray climbed inside and looked around. He slammed the door shut and locked it. He said, "Everyone gets on the floor."

People started to murmur fearfully but followed orders and lowered themselves to the floor. Once they were down, he, too, sat. Then he said in a whisper, "I hope you know what you're doing, Jake."

So did Hawk. Upon reaching the roof, he found the automatic braking system and said a little prayer as he used his belt to fasten himself to the roof. Then he aimed the 433 and fired.

At first, nothing happened. Then the cable car began to inch forward. Slowly, at first, before starting to pick up speed. This wasn't too bad, Hawk thought to himself. A lot better than anticipated.

But the forces of gravity were at work on the car, and it picked up speed, traveling faster and faster until it reached a breakneck pace.

"Fucking stupid thing to do," Hawk growled, picturing his death at the other end.

Meanwhile, inside the car, fear and panic was in full swing and growing. Several of the women were screaming, and one of the men asked loudly, "Is it meant to go this fast?"

"Just shut up and hang on, mate," Gray said. "We'll stop soon."

Fucking suddenly.

The wind whipped past Hawk's face, the cold biting at his exposed skin. In the distance, he could see the other cable car house. Before, it was a concrete apron and before that, a large snow drift. He had an idea.

If he stayed where he was, he'd die. It was that simple. "Man, I hope there are no rocks."

Hawk untied himself and he waited until the last possible moment and threw himself from the roof of the cable car. He hit the snow drift at an enormous pace, and as he did, everything went black.

Meanwhile, the rocket that was the car came to a screeching halt inside the cable car house. The people inside were thrown around like salad in a stir fry. Gray crashed into something soft and heard someone cry out in pain.

There was a moment of silence, albeit brief, before someone started to cry out in pain. That voice was joined by another, and another as the shock of the impact wore off. The lights inside the cable car house were still on, illuminating the inside of the car. Gray shook his head to clear the cobwebs and looked around him. The people against the leading wall had taken the brunt of the impact. Those like himself were cushioned by the bodies in between.

Gray got to his feet and started checking the girls they had rescued. All were able to walk. One had a broken arm, two maybe broken ribs. Lucky compared to some of the guests who had pushed their way at the top. Two of them were dead.

Gray got his charges out and as an afterthought, remembered Hawk. "Shit. One, are you okay?"

There was no response. Hawk wasn't on the roof, nor was he plastered across the cable car house like some sticky condiment. "Mucker, where are you? Talk to me."

"I'm here," came Hawk's voice.

Gray turned and saw Hawk standing in the doorway. His clothes looked torn, and there was blood on his left shoulder. "Are you okay?" Gray asked.

"Better than I would have been if I'd stayed on for the grand finale. What about you and the girls?"

"A little banged up, but they'll make it."

"We need to find a ride and get the hell out of here to Pavel."

They found a truck. More exactly, a Vityaz—ATV. A vehicle used by the Russian armed forces. "Can you drive this thing?" Gray asked Hawk.

"How hard can it be?"

Suddenly, an explosion rocked the night. They looked up at the castle and saw the orange fireball rising into the sky.

"Bloody hell," Gray said.

"Come on, let's get out of here."

Getting the girls loaded on board, Gray checked them over while they were on the move. One young waif-like girl with haunted eyes looked at him and asked, "Are you really going to take us home?"

The former para nodded. "That's the plan."

"I feel so fuzzy."

"That's the drugs. Just close your eyes and rest. Let me and my mate worry about the other stuff."

"You are British?" another girl asked.

"Yes."

Having checked each girl over thoroughly, Gray moved back to the front. "How are they looking?" Hawk asked.

"They'll be right until we get them proper medical attention." There was a pause. "We were lucky, Jake."

"Yeah. Don't tell Ilse."

———————

ILSE PUNCHED him in the arm. "You are a bloody pillock."

"Ease up, it wasn't that bad."

"Yeah, it was," Gray said. "Especially the part where we free-fell with the cable car."

Ilse stared at Hawk open-mouthed. "What?"

"It wasn't a free fall. More an uncontrolled descent," Hawk assured her. "We were still attached to the cable."

"Barely."

"You both shouldn't have been in that situation in the first place," Anja said grimly.

"We got the girls," Hawk pointed out.

"You both could have died when you were told not to. What part of *observe only* did you not understand?"

"Well, at least we can confirm the Silver Fox is dead. And his lair is no more."

"Why did she kill her father?" Ilse asked.

"She didn't agree with what he was doing. Saw him as a traitor to their country."

The Marabou lurched as it hit some turbulence. They were headed to Rome, where on the outskirts of the city, there was a private airfield which could accommodate the plane. Once there, they would pass the girls over to the authorities who would then debrief each and return them to their homes.

"We still need to find her and take her out," Slania said.

"Any luck in tracking the helicopter?" Hawk asked.

"No, we lost it. But rest assured, we'll find her."

Anja said, "People and organizations like this always have a backup center of operations. That's where she will be headed. Somewhere, she can hide and regroup. Find that, and we locate her."

"That could take a while," Ilse said.

"They mentioned something about a brother before she killed her father," Hawk said. "Get this, stupidity runs in the family. He calls himself the Pale Crow."

"Dig into it, Slania. Ilse will help you."

"What do we do until then?" Hawk asked.

"We are going home to Santorini. We need a break."

"I won't complain about that," Gray said.

Anja nodded. "Good. We'll drop the girls off and then head to our little piece of paradise."

Which is what they did.

"REPORTS ARE THAT THEY ESCAPED," Vadim said to Svetlana.

"They are like fucking cockroaches," she hissed. "A fucking nuclear weapon won't even kill them."

"We didn't use a nuclear weapon."

"You know what I mean."

The woman known as the White Dove lay next to a pool filled with crystal clear water. The warm sun touched her exposed skin not covered by her white bikini. She reached for the drink on the table. Vodka and ice. A small droplet of condensation dripped onto her flat stomach. It was cold, and goose flesh sprung up as her skin reacted to the cold. Even her nipples hardened beneath the tight fabric.

"Was there something else?" Svetlana asked.

Vadim averted his eyes, checking the three armed guards. All carried AKs. Each of them looked outward across the beach below and the azure waters. One of Morocco's best qualities.

"We need to find another way of acquiring girls for the businesses."

"Have you any suggestions?"

"Well—"

"Spit it out. If you have an idea, I'm listening."

"Your brother."

"No." Her one-word answer held a definite edge.

Vadim pressed the issue. "He has contacts and the means of doing it."

"He is an arrogant asshole who I want nothing to do with."

"Then what do you suggest?" Vadim asked curtly.

The tone hadn't gone unnoticed. "Remember who you speak to, Vadim."

"I apologize, Svetlana, but we can't sit around here and do nothing. If we do, money is wasted."

"I am aware of that. Find me Kurt Runciman. I want to talk to him."

Vadim hesitated.

"What?"

"Runciman is more of a liability," Vadim explained. "He kidnaps openly with violence. Not like Declan and his people. Using Runciman is like putting up a flare in a storm."

"He will do until we can find something better. When you find him, set up a video call."

"As you wish."

LATER THAT EVENING, Svetlana accepted a call from Kurt Runciman, the face staring back from her screen looking more like a professional night-clubber than an acquisitions specialist. With blond streaks in his black hair, round rose-colored glasses, and striped coat. "Svetlana, it has been a while. I heard about your father. I am sorry for your loss."

"It happens."

"I also heard about Declan. I take it that this is a business call."

"It is."

"Then your wish is my command. What would you like.?"

"I have a very rich Italian who is looking for a toy. Not just any toy, mind, something exquisite."

Runciman chuckled.

"What is so funny, Kurt?" Svetlana asked.

"The way you talk about your fellow ladies. It makes them sound like sides of meat."

"This is business, Kurt. Feelings have no place in it. If you have a problem, then I will find someone else."

Runciman shook his head. "There is no need. What were you thinking?"

"At the Rome University of Fine Arts, there is a young lady who might fit the needs of my customer," Svetlana informed him.

"That is more than a little risky," Runciman pointed out. "The proper practice would be to pick the fruit from a different country. Preferably one that is thousands of miles away."

"The one I have chosen isn't thousands of miles away. She is in Rome."

"What about the buyer?"

"Bologna."

Runciman let out a sigh.

"Do you want the job or not, Kurt?" Svetlana asked.

"How much?"

"I will pay five-hundred thousand."

"Who is the target?"

"Amara Al-Fayrouz," Svetlana replied as her picture appeared.

There was a long silence as Runciman stared at the image on the screen. Svetlana could see his mind ticking over. "Can you do it?"

"Of course, I can do it. The question is, do I want to kidnap a princess from the bloody UAE? She will have armed bodyguards as her security detail. It could get messy."

"Last I heard was five, but you need to decide."

"Fine, I will do it. But I need to make the hand-off right away. I cannot hold something like this."

"I will have it arranged."

"Good, then I will take the job for another five hundred."

"That is a lot of money, Kurt."

"That is a lot of women, and I bet you are getting a lot more than one million for the girl, Svetlana."

"All right, I will pay it. Half up front, the rest on receipt."

"Done. I will let you know when we are about to move so the customer can be ready."

"I will await your call."

Svetlana looked up from the screen. "Well?"

Vadim remained stoic. "I still think this is a mistake, Svetlana."

"I guess time will tell. Now, do you wish to sleep with me tonight or not? I need something to help me relax."

"Your wish is my command."

CHAPTER NINETEEN

"I COULD GET USED to staying at home," Hawk said as he adjusted his sunglasses and took a pull of his beer.

Slania was in the pool, leaning against the side while Ilse was in a red bikini, lounging on an inflatable mattress, catching rays. Gray was out on another beer run while Anja was doing Anja things. Working on intel.

"I heard that the Reaper lives around here some-where," Slania said.

"He's got himself a setup on Iraklia," Hawk said. "It's about a hundred and thirty klicks from here. His sister lives there with him."

"I heard he was a serious operator."

"And then some."

"Better than you?"

"I'd leave room for three at the top of that tree," Hawk said.

"Oh, who's the third?"

"A former SAS guy called Ray Jensen. His friends call him *Knocker*."

"He was the one who recruited you for the task force, wasn't he?" Ilse asked.

"Yes, that's him."

"He's a bit of a stud."

"He'd eat you alive, babe. More wives than hot dinners."

"What's his problem?" Slania asked.

"He's married to his work," Hawk replied.

"Aren't you hot?" Ilse asked him.

"I was just starting to think that," Hawk replied and got up. He walked over to the pool and slipped in. The cool water enveloped him as he took a dip, keeping his bottle above the water as he came to the surface. Wiping the droplets from his eyes, he felt better already.

Hawk waded over to where Ilse lay on the mattress. He dabbed the cold bottle of beer onto her flat stomach, and she jerked, her skin pimpled from the cool. "Schuft!"

Hawk grinned, standing erect and leaning in to kiss her. Then he settled back into the water.

"I come bearing gifts," Gray announced as he appeared with more beer.

"Shit," Hawk moaned. "You got the wrong brand."

"That was all they had. They're waiting on supplies."

"I like it," Ilse said as she slipped into the water behind Hawk and wrapped her arms around him. "Maybe even better than you, my sweet."

"Fine. Given over for a beer. That's okay."

She kissed him on the cheek and waded over to Gray, an arm extended. "Beer. Now."

"Have you left him?"

"Give me a beer and I'm all yours."

Hawk turned. "Slania?"

"Fuck off. Give me a beer, Marcus."

Hawk nodded. "Great."

After spending another hour in the pool, the sun began to drop, and they all climbed out. Everyone showered before meeting up in the kitchen to cook the main meal. It was something they all participated in during their downtime. Even Anja joined them.

"What are we having tonight?" she asked.

"Chicken," Ilse said.

"What kind?"

"I'm not sure. Any ideas?"

"I know a great marinade recipe," Anja replied.

"All right, then, lead the way, boss."

"Marcus, grab me a beer, please. This will be thirsty work."

An hour later they were gathered around the table like a large family eating the chicken that Anja cooked. "This is good food, boss," Hawk said as he shoveled the chicken in.

"I'm glad you like it, Jacob."

"What's not to like? Sauce, meat, veggies—well, maybe not veggies. All we're missing is a bottle of wine."

"Look around you, Jake," Anja said. "Do we look like wine drinkers to you?"

The men wore shorts and tank tops and the women bikinis. Even Anja. He shook his head. "Yeah, nah."

"Anything in the wind, boss?" Gray asked.

Everyone moaned and put their cutlery down. Slania stared at him across the table. "You just had to do it. Couldn't go one day without talking about work."

"Bloody pillock," Hawk growled.

"That's it, I'm leaving you for Jake. At least he has some sense."

"Why thank you," Hawk replied.

Anja smiled. "Seeing as the egg has been cracked, make the most of tonight. Tomorrow, we go back to work."

Slania glared at Gray. "Asshole."

"Where to, boss?" Hawk asked.

"Austria. Salzburg, to be precise. Our friend the Pale Crow is there."

"Good grief, I'll never get used to that name," Gray said. "It is so lame."

"What are we going to do with him?" Hawk asked.

"Pick him up, have a chat."

"What does he do?" Ilse asked.

"Anything that is illegal," Anja replied. "He runs with a four-man bodyguard unit."

"Some would say that's not enough."

"We'll see."

———

"ARE we still catch and release, boss?" Hawk asked Anja.

"Affirmative. Your package will arrive at the coffee house at ten."

Hawk looked at his watch. It was 9:55 a.m. "I hope the intel is good."

Hawk and Gray were in a white cargo van with Ilse behind the wheel. The plan was to wait until the right moment, disable the target's bodyguard, and then make off with him. The coffee shop they had staked out was on a narrow one-way street with baroque architecture on each side.

Both Hawk and Gray were armed with handheld tasers that would disable the bodyguards without killing them. But, if things went pear-shaped, they were both still carrying their SIGs.

Ilse was looking in the side mirror when she said, "Heads up."

A black BMW SUV drove past them and pulled up in the empty space outside the coffee shop. They sat and watched as three men climbed out. "I see the target," Ilse said.

"We're two short," Gray noted.

"I'm not going to complain," Hawk said. "Let's go and have a coffee."

Getting out of the van, the pair struck up a casual conversation as they walked along the sidewalk before entering the coffee shop. The smell of coffee was strong within. Hawk looked around and saw Sergei Orlov sitting with his bodyguards at a table near the window. There was a spare table behind them. "Perfect," Hawk muttered.

"I'll get the coffees," Gray said.

While he did so, Hawk went to the table and sat down.

Sergei was talking on his cell. His two bodyguards were lazy, chatting to each other rather than looking for threats. Maybe they were too used to Sergei's reputation, with most people scared of him. After all, anyone who crossed Sergei would be found dead in a dumpster or a waterway.

But Hawk and Gray weren't just anyone. Gray was good, Hawk was better. These two were useless.

Gray walked over carrying the coffees and a white paper sack of pastries, and sat down. "Well?"

"These pricks are half asleep. We'll get them on the way out."

"Roger that."

Removing the pastries from the bag, Hawk and Gray began to enjoy the buttery texture with their coffees. "What are you two doing?" Ilse asked over their comms.

"Just enjoying the cuisine," Hawk replied quietly.

"Great. You two are living it up while I'm out here entertaining myself."

"Don't have too much fun," Hawk replied.

"We're moving," Gray said, cutting off the conversation.

Rising from their seats, they started out the door behind the target. As Hawk expected, Sergei's men were

231

lazy. They'd been doing their job for too long. It allowed the two Talon men to come up behind them and hit them with the tasers.

The bodyguards dropped to the sidewalk like stones, and before Sergei realized what was happening, Gray had hit him, and he was in Hawk's arms.

The cargo van roared as Ilse pulled up beside them. Gray slid the door open, and they bundled the Russian inside. Following him into the cargo space, by the time Ilse had pulled away from the sidewalk, Hawk and Gray had the target secure.

Hawk sat with his back against the van wall. "And that, my friends, is how you do it."

THE SCENE RESEMBLED A WAR ZONE. As Runciman walked toward the SUV with the target inside, he shot one of the wounded bodyguards in the head. Svetlana's intel had been fucked up. Amara had been attended by ten bodyguards.

All were now lying in pools of their own blood on the street, just as some of Runciman's men were. He was far from happy with the outcome, but the extra money made it worth it. His crew were armed with Heckler and Koch G36 assault rifles. The bodyguards had been outgunned.

Runciman drew closer to the SUV. It was armored and bore many scars, testament to the heavy fire it had sustained. No holes. On the inside, Amara was hunkered down on the floor in the back. Runciman knocked on the window. "Open the door."

"Go away."

"Come on, Amara, we can do this the easy way, or the hard way. It is your choice."

232

"Go away!" she repeated, but this time, she pointed a handgun at him and pulled the trigger.

The glass, of course, was bulletproof, and the bullet ricocheted off it and buried itself in the upholstery of the SUV. Runciman held up his hands. "Whoa, don't do that, you'll kill yourself."

The ricochet frightened Amara, and she dropped the handgun but didn't open the door.

"Last chance, Amara." Runciman looked around. Almost all civilians in the area had scattered. But there was always one. That single person who thought filming the action was going to make them famous. And there he was, phone up, filming it all. "Fucking idiot."

Runciman raised his weapon and shot the wannabe director.

Inside the SUV, Amara screamed. By now, Runciman's patience had run out, and he placed a breaching charge on the door and stepped away. The following blast dislodged the door and knocked Amara senseless. Runciman waved at two of his men. "Get her."

They dragged the girl free of the SUV without any resistance and then bundled her into one of their waiting vehicles. Now that the hard part was done, all they had to do was make the delivery.

———

THE ROOM they were in was sterile. Sergei sat on one side of the table, Hawk and Anja on the other. Bound in chains, Sergei was going nowhere. The first words out of his mouth were, "You cannot do this." They were followed by, "Do you know who I am?"

To which Hawk replied, "A piece of dog shit that has been spread across the street, wiped up, and fucking laid down again."

"I will kill you."

Hawk grinned. "Go ahead, sonny. I eat shite like you for breakfast."

"We'll—"

"Oh, shut up," Anja growled at the Russian. "If you ever want to get out of this room then you will help us by answering our questions."

"I will give you nothing," Sergei spat defiantly, the look on his face pure hatred.

Anja stood up. "Then we have nothing more to discuss. Call Interpol and hand him over."

"Boss."

They stood up. "Wait!"

When they turned to stare at Sergei, his visage was now panicked, contrite. He said, "What do you want to know?"

"Did you know that your father is dead?" Anja asked, sitting back down.

The Russian nodded. "Yes. I heard."

"We are looking for your sister. Do you have any idea where she might be?"

"Why would I know? If you can't tell, my sister and I don't see eye to eye on anything."

"Was there any particular place that your father used to go? Holidays off the grid? A backup just in case anything went wrong?"

"I don't know, they changed all the time."

"Were there any that didn't?" Hawk asked. "Maybe a favorite?"

"There was one place," Sergei said thoughtfully. "In Morocco."

There was a knock on the door, and Ilse entered, a tablet in her hand which she passed to Anja. It was paused on a video. Anja hit play and watched until it stopped. She stood up. "Everyone out."

Once outside the room, Anja asked, "Where was this taken?"

"Rome, a couple of hours ago."

Anja gave the tablet to Hawk, and while the others talked, he watched. The Talon commander asked, "Who was the target?"

"Amara Al-Fayrouz."

"Was this Svetlana and her people?"

"No," Hawk said. "This is the work of Kurt Runciman."

"Which means?" Anja asked.

"He's like Declan Hunter, only messier. Actually, he's a blunt instrument."

"Kidnap for hire," Ilse muttered.

"He has to be working for someone then," Anja said.

"It will be Svetlana," Hawk replied. "We took out her go-to guy, now she needs another to fill the void. He's not her usual thing, but beggars can't be choosers at the moment."

"Then we go after Runciman," Ilse said.

"No," Anja replied. "Find out where Amara was taken. Someone that important, they won't hold her for long. We get the customer, then maybe we get the supplier."

"We still need to get Runciman at some point, boss," Hawk pointed out.

"We will, but that is for another day."

"What about Sergei?"

"Let Interpol have him."

———

"BOSS, I HAVE THE CUSTOMER," Slania said to Anja. It had taken twenty-four hours, but Slania had done it.

235

"Get everyone together."

Minutes later, Slania was briefing the team. "Bruno Asti. Head of the Asti Crime Family. Divorced by bullet."

"Someone murdered his wife?" Hawk asked curiously.

"Yes. He did. Can't be proven, though."

"I'm going to love talking to him. Kids?"

"None."

"Bruno dabbles in illicit substances. By that, I mean he's a major importer." The large screen changed from a photo to a video feed. "This was taken from his security feed in Bologna."

"Is that Amara?" Gray asked.

"We think so," Anja confirmed.

"Have you notified Italian authorities?"

"No. This is ours to prosecute. If they pick him up, we don't get to ask the questions we need answered."

"But what if he—you know?" Hawk asked. "She'll never be able to go back home."

"It's a chance I'm willing to take," Anja replied. "If something terrible does happen then she will be relocated. I hope it doesn't, which is why we're leaving right now. Slania will get you what you need to plan a hard insert."

"Sounds good," Hawk said.

"Jake," Ilse admonished him.

"What? I was just saying that a hard insert sounds good. It's to our advantage."

"Uh, huh."

"Gear up on the plane. All of what you need is on it. We fly as soon as we get there."

———

A FULL CONTINGENT of guards were deployed on the grounds. It was dark, Slania had disabled the motion sensors, and the security feed was on a loop. However, it

236

wouldn't hold for too long, so Hawk and Gray had to move fast.

Their NVGs were useless due to all the floodlit areas. They were wearing their body armor and their Synoprathetic suits. Their main weapon of choice was a Heckler and Koch MP5SD.

"X-ray down," Hawk whispered as he moved forward. He stepped over the body and kept making his way through the garden.

"Roger," Slania said. "As soon as you reach the house, I'll cut the power."

"No, leave it on. We need to make a positive ID on the target."

There was a guard by the pool, and another by the pool house. The high number of security could only be due to Amara's presence.

Using hand signals, Hawk and Gray picked their targets and lined their weapons up ready for the kill. "Now."

Both fired, and the two guards dropped with a dull thud.

Once again, they were moving. As they were pushing past a large, double-glazed floor-to-ceiling window it suddenly exploded outward. Gunfire tore through it, filling the air with glass. The rest of the window fell like a curtain of rain to reveal the shooter standing inside the living room.

Gray whipped his MP5 around and opened fire. The shooter staggered and fell back. Now that the door was open, the pair went inside, not bothering to wipe their feet.

Gray led, and as soon as he stepped into the room, another figure appeared. He was armed and already firing. The rattle of the automatic weapon sounded almost deafening. A short burst from Gray sent bullets hammering into the shooter's chest. He cried out and fell to the floor, hitting the sofa on the way down.

Another shooter stepped in to replace his fallen comrade, firing a Beretta PMX. It seemed to chew its way through the magazine in a wild display of firepower. Bullets punched into walls and cut through the air, searching for a target. Both Talon operators dived behind the sofa.

"Shoot the prick," Hawk snarled as bullets punched through the fabric and foam.

"Shoot the bastard yourself."

"Shit," Hawk growled. "You want something done, you have to do it your fucking self."

Rolling from behind the sofa, Hawk came up onto his knees, flicking the selector on his weapon around to full auto.

He squeezed the trigger, and the MP5 disgorged the rest of its magazine. The shooter started a macabre dance as the rounds peppered his torso, spraying blood across the room. "Now fuck off."

With the immediate threats neutralized, they jumped to their feet and headed for the doorway into the hallway. Gray stepped through and jerked back as a shooter fired along the narrow corridor. "Shit."

Gray poked the MP5 around the corner and fired a long burst. A cry of pain indicated that another Italian killer was gone.

"The library is on the far side of the front entry," Ilse said. "There is someone there."

Hawk took point as they hurried along the hallway toward the front of the house. Yet another shooter appeared. This one from behind them. Gray had been watching rear security, and as soon as the shooter appeared, he fired.

"Far out, how many men does this guy have?"

Hawk and Gray reached the main foyer and found the door which led through to the library. "Is he inside?" Hawk asked quietly.

"I'm not going to say it is him, Bravo One, but it is someone."

Gray tried the door. Gunfire erupted from within, and bullets blew through the thin veneer. Hawk reached for a stun grenade. Gray opened the door wide enough to send it through. Hawk pulled the pin and tossed it.

Moments later, the stun grenade detonated. Hawk burst through, shoving the door wide. The shooter on the other side was staggering around, the grenade having done its work. Within seconds, the shooter was on the floor. Hawk rolled him over and nodded. "Alpha, we have the target. Continuing to target two."

"Roger. Be aware there are still at least two more shooters converging on the house."

Gray dragged Bruno to his feet. "Where is the girl?"

"What girl?" he hissed.

The former para let his weapon hang and smashed a fist into Bruno's face. "The girl."

"Fuck you."

Suddenly, a shooter stepped through the doorway. Hawk reacted instantly and shot the man in the leg. He collapsed to the floor in pain. Hawk was on him before he could recover. The former SAS operator kicked the wounded man's weapon away and dragged him over to lie in front of Bruno.

Hawk grabbed his P320 and pointed it at the newcomer's head. "Where is the girl?"

The wounded man glanced at Bruno and then spat at Hawk. Moments later, a bullet punched into his brain.

"Right," Hawk said to Bruno. "As you can see, I'm through fucking around. Now, where is the girl?"

The man said nothing.

The gun came up.

"Wait! She is in the basement."

"Lead the way."

He got cautiously to his feet before heading down the hall to the stairs that led to the basement. It resembled a large dungeon, custom-built for the millionaire. The floors were marble, and the cages were hardened plastic or glass. The walls were granite, and each cell had a proper bed with other items of leisure. Hawk considered the possibility that at some point, each of these cells could have been occupied. It would have been horrifying.

At the end of the rows of cells was a larger cell. The glass was opaque. They could not see what was beyond the exterior. Bruno walked over to a column on the wall and pressed a button.

The glass became instantly clear, and they could finally see what had been concealed.

The room was similar to the others but larger and with added extras like a four-poster bed, spa bath, and luxurious wall adornments. And there, sitting on the edge of the bed, looking tired, was Amara Al-Fayrouz.

There was a noise behind them, and without any hesitation, Hawk turned, raised his P320, and fired at the last security guard that had found them. The bullet hit him in the head, and he fell to the hard floor.

Hawk turned and focused his burning gaze on Bruno. "Open the fucking cell."

Bruno pressed another button, and the front of the cell slid open. Gray slipped inside and approached the woman. She flinched, fear in her eyes.

"Are you Amara Al-Fayrouz?" Gray asked her.

She looked at him, confused. "What?"

"Are you Amara Al-Fayrouz?" His voice was gentle but firm.

"Yes, I am."

"You need to come with us, Miss. We're going to take you out of here."

She got unsteadily to her feet. "Just stand there, ma'am, I need to check you out. Did they give you anything?"

"Yes—no—oh, I don't know."

"They gave her something, Jake," Gray said, reaching for his compact medical kit.

"What did you give her?" Hawk asked Bruno.

"Just a general sedative."

"Did you get that, Marcus?"

"Yeah." Gray looked at Amara as he took out a hypodermic and said, "Just relax, this will help."

"What are you—"

It was over before Amara knew what was happening.

"She should be good, Jake."

"Okay, let's get out of here." Hawk paused. He turned to the Italian. "I'd like to put a fucking bullet in your little brain, but you've got too many questions to answer. But if you try to escape, I'll bury you right here, right fucking now. Do you understand?"

He nodded.

"Alpha, this is Bravo, we're coming home."

CHAPTER TWENTY

THE TEAM WAS STILL in Italy, awaiting Slania and Ilse to gather more intelligence that might provide an answer to the one question they still hadn't resolved. Where was Svetlana?

"Morocco."

All heads turned to Anja. Hawk asked, "How sure, boss?"

"Almost one hundred percent," she replied. "While we've been working, she's been living it up in the sun."

"Great. How soon before we can act?"

"I've already got twenty-four-hour surveillance on the estate. If she's there, we'll know, and if she leaves, we'll know that too. Until then, act like she is, draw up a plan, and be ready to execute it."

"I only have one question, boss," Hawk said. "Is this an extract or targeted assassination?"

"If you can't extract, you have a green light to terminate. The woman is a clear and present global danger."

"Roger that," Hawk replied. He glanced at Slania. "We're going to need some of your best work."

"Don't you always?"

"And we get it."

Anja nodded. "Okay, get to it, coordinate all that you need."

"Boss, do you want me to reach out to the Moroccan government?" Ilse asked. "They might get a little pissy if we just go in."

"Do you have someone you trust in Moroccan Intelligence?"

"Yes."

"Go through them. I don't want our silver bird tipped off at the eleventh hour."

"Roger that."

Anja turned to Slania. "Let me know whatever you need. Same with you, Jake. Mary Thurston can help if we aren't able to get it."

The team began dispersing, setting about their assigned tasks. Slania supplied Hawk and Gray with an intel package, and the pair of operators went to work.

———

"THE VILLA IS NOT on the water but close enough for a wet insertion," Hawk said to Gray.

The former para shook his head. "They will be expecting it. I say HALO insert."

Hawk nodded. He was good with that. "Okay. Maybe helicopter extract."

"Sounds right. We'll need a platform offshore. In and out before Moroccan authorities can get on-site. If they get hold of Svetlana, we'll lose her for sure."

"We have to make sure that doesn't happen," Hawk said. "We put her down no matter what."

"No matter what."

"Now, let's have a look at this villa. The usual suspects. Pool, outdoor dining, two pool houses."

"For the bodyguard, I'd say, Jake."

Hawk nodded. "Yes. Vinyard. You see that gully going through the center? Might make a good insertion point."

Gray picked up the photo. "There looks to be a good LZ about a click out. Nice and flat."

Hawk looked at it. "Okay, we know how we're getting in."

"Do we have something with guard positions?"

They shuffled through the photographs. Hawk shook his head. "Nothing as yet. Wait, One."

He took out his cell and punched a button. Ilse answered on the other end. "Does Slania have anything regarding security positions?"

"Why don't you ask her?" Ilse answered sharply.

"I just wanted to hear your voice," Hawk replied.

"What about my voice, Mr. Hawk?" Anja asked.

"Am I on speaker?"

"Idiot," Ilse said.

"I'll just call Slania."

"Don't waste your time, Jake," Slania said. She was there too.

"You lot are taking the piss, aren't you?" Hawk growled. Ilse started to chuckle. "This was a bloody stitch-up."

"What do you need, Jake?" Slania asked.

"I need security positions."

"I think I have something. Be right there."

But it was Ilse who showed up instead of Slania. The grin on her face told them everything they needed to know. She handed over the photo and kissed Hawk on the head. "You're a moron."

"You should be apologizing to me," he replied. "You set me up."

She stepped closer to him, her hand on his shoulder. Hawk, in return, wrapped his arm around her waist and slipped his hand into the back pocket of her jeans. Ilse asked, "Where are we at?"

"We'll need a HALO insert platform and a helicopter extract." Hawk touched the flat area on the photo. "We'll use this as our LZ so we can get on target as quick as possible. Come up through this gully."

"What about the fence?"

"Never let a little obstacle get in your way. What about those guards, Mucker?"

"Five."

"Five? Be fucked."

"Count them yourself," Gray said.

Hawk freed his hand from the denim trap and leaned forward. He counted, frowned, and then counted again. He looked up at Ilse. "Can you get Slania to doublecheck this?"

"Waste of time, Jake. She would have already done so."

"That's not enough," Hawk said. "That is nowhere near enough."

"Maybe that's all she has," Ilse said.

"Not on your bloody life."

Hawk flicked through the other photos until he found one that was zoomed out. He stabbed the photo with a crooked finger. "We need eyes on this adjacent estate. I need to know what is in it."

"Do you think there are more security personnel there?"

"If there are, I want to know. If not, then why?"

The following day as things were coming together, Hawk got his answer. "They are hooked in with the police. Nothing like paying out a lot of money for support."

"It's something we'll have to deal with."

Anja entered. "Are you ready, Jake?"

"I guess we are, boss."

"Good. If all goes well, you head tomorrow night. It's time to finish the final chapter in this bloody book for good."

———

MAKING it onto the designated LZ without any problems, it was dark, and they moved into position in the gully, preparing to commence their assault. Both Gray and Hawk carried their standard suppressed HK 433s.

Once the fence was cut, they called in. "Alpha, copy?"

"We see you, Bravo," came the reply.

The team was on a freighter offshore with a UAV on watch. The Moroccan government had given them a two-hour window to get the mission completed. If not, they would move their own people in. Which was ridiculous because the police were in it up to their eyeballs.

"We're moving in."

"Roger that. All motion sensors have been disabled. Take the guards at the rear of the house first."

"Roger," Hawk replied.

He and Gray slipped through the fence. Using the garden for cover as they'd done so many times before, they were able to creep within a good range of the guards at the back of the villa. Both men brought up their weapons and took a target each.

"Execute." Hawk's voice was barely a whisper.

Fingers stroked their triggers, and two bullets found their targets. Both guards fell. "Two X-rays down."

"Okay, target on the pool side of the villa."

Gray disappeared ahead of Hawk through the thicker undergrowth of the garden. If you're going to be a crook and have a garden, make sure that it is open and can't be used for all kinds of cover.

Gray came to a halt among some roses and brought his weapon up. The third guard was pacing across the sandstone pavers past a large glass-fronted pool house with doors at its center. He waited. If he missed the target, the sound of shattering glass would act like an alarm.

Gray watched the guard pause, unsure what he was about to do, but after a few moments, the man kept walking. As soon as he cleared the glass background, Gray dropped him.

"Third X-ray down."

"Right, you have the two at the front door and you're clear for insert."

"Status?" Gray asked.

"One target upstairs, and the second downstairs in a living area."

"Copy."

Hawk caught up with Gray. "We all good, Mucker?"

"Just the lads at the front door," Gray replied.

The pair began moving back through the garden, circling around toward the front. The two remaining guards looked to be imitating the Roman pillars on which they were leaning. Once again, the two Brits brought up their weapons and with precision, eliminated the threats.

"Alpha, we're good at the front. Moving to breach."

"Copy, Bravo. Targets remain the same."

Hawk said, "Up or down?"

"A gentleman is always hesitant to sneak into a lady's bedroom," Gray said with an upper class tone.

Hawk grunted. "Good thing I'm not a fucking gentleman."

Hawk tried the door, and it opened easily. Inside, the foyer was clear of life. He walked toward the stairs laid in terracotta tiles. Gray made a move toward the living room.

Taking the stairs quickly but quietly, Hawk reached the landing before starting along a hallway adorned with green plants in terracotta pots.

"First room on the left, Bravo," Ilse said.

Hawk lowered his 433 and took out the suppressed P320. He held out his hand to turn the knob, and with sudden violence, the door came free of its hinges and crashed into him.

———

MEANWHILE, Gray was entering the living room. He swept left and right and saw nothing. In his ear, he heard Ilse say, "Talk to me, Bravo Two."

"It looks all clear."

"Say again."

"The room is all clear."

"Negative Two, I say again, negative, the room is not clear. Target left."

A sudden crash rocked the villa, and Gray looked up. That was when Svetlana hit him with two shots in the chest. With a grunt of pain, Gray went down and didn't move.

Svetlana appeared from the shadows, a gun in her hand. She stood over the former para and sneered, "You should be more careful."

Then she raised the gun and pointed it at Gray. Hesitating, she wondered whether a third shot was actually necessary.

———

HAWK STAGGERED backward into the wall. The meat in a brutal sandwich. The wall, then him, then the door, and last, Vadim. The former SAS operator let out a cry of pain as it ripped through his body. He fell sideways, the P320 releasing from his grasp.

The door fell on Hawk as he hit the floor. Vadim reached down and threw it easily aside. He grabbed a handful of Hawk's clothing and dragged him upright. Hawk took one blurred look and snarled, "My mother should have fucking raised me better."

He lashed out at the face before him. Although his fist made contact, he was still recovering, and his blow was lacking. Vadim hit Hawk flush, and he crashed to the floor once more. Hawk shook his head to clear the cobwebs. He grinned. "You'll have to do better than that, Ivan."

"My name is Vadim," Vadim snapped and reached down to drag Hawk erect once more.

This time, Hawk was waiting.

As the Russian came down, Hawk's boot came up. He hit Vadim in the chest and sent the killer reeling. Hawk scrambled to his feet and followed the big man. Vadim crashed against the wall.

Hawk unleashed a couple of straight rights to the Russian's face. The blows rocked Vadim, but he had nowhere to go. Hawk hit him again.

The Talon operator moved closer and swung hard. This time, Vadim responded. But not in the way Hawk had expected. Reaching out, he grasped a nearby vase, swinging it in a broad arc and smashing it into Hawk's head dislodging his helmet.

Hawk staggered, blood starting to flow freely from a cut to his head. Vadim snorted. "You bleed, little man."

"Not that fucking little," Hawk responded.

Vadim rushed him. His shoulder hit Hawk, driving him back along the hallway. They crashed through a side table and another vase, this one containing flowers, fell and shattered on the floor.

Hawk kept lashing out, and for the first time, he realized that if he didn't finish it quickly he might not finish it at all.

Vadim hit him between the eyes. His head bounced, and stars flashed through his brain. The big killer reached for his throat, large fingers starting to lock on. Hawk's hand shuffled around looking for a weapon. At first, there was nothing. Then he found something.

The Talon operator's right hand came up with as much power as he could muster. The shard of shattered pottery stabbed into Vadim's eye. It collected part of the socket before entering then encountered resistance. It should have gone to the brain. It didn't.

Vadim reared back, roaring like a bear. He hit the wall and slid sideways, clawing at his face before pulling the bloody shard free, leaving an ugly hole.

The big Russian threw it aside and lurched to his feet. With another loud roar he came forward, all caution gone. Hawk stood, waiting for the impact. Then, just as the Russian was about to hit, Hawk brought up his right fist and hit him in the throat. Not once, but twice, the last blow seeming to skid off to the side.

Vadim stopped abruptly, staring at the knife in Hawk's hand. Alarm flashed through his eyes, and as he looked down, he could see that his shirt had become a flooding sea of red.

He fell to his knees, the light in his eyes starting to fade. Then, like a tree in the forest, Vadim fell and would never rise again.

———

SVETLANA WAS STANDING TOO CLOSE. She thought Gray was dead. After all, she'd shot him twice in the chest. But why was there no blood?

Gray's leg swept both of hers from beneath her. Svet-

250

lana crashed to the hard floor. The former para came to his feet with a loud groan. "You take too long to make fucking decisions, you bloody cow."

Svetlana scooted backward and came up into a crouch. "I don't know how you are still alive," she hissed.

"It's called a Synoprathetic suit."

The woman came out of her crouch like a panther, but turned instantly into a professional ballerina, pirouetting, bringing a powerful leg up and around, her heel catching Gray on the cheek.

He staggered backward, tasting blood inside his mouth. Svetlana immediately followed him, throwing a couple punches which Gray blocked successfully before stepping back. There was a wild catlike rage in Svetlana's eyes. Her hands were hooked like claws.

The enraged trafficker swung another kick at Gray which he blocked. He grabbed her ankle and dragged her close. His clenched fist hit her hard in the solar plexus, and he heard the rush of air. Gray released her foot, and Svetlana doubled over.

Walking over to her, Gray wrapped her slender throat in his right hand.

"Had enough?"

She spat at him.

He brought his forehead in savagely and headbutted her.

Blood flowed from her cut nose as she lurched back free of the grasp. Svetlana sat down hard on the sofa. Gray walked over to her. Something caught her eye. The solid crystal ashtray on the coffee table.

With a loud screech, she grabbed it and threw the object hard. Gray responded reflexively but not fast enough. It caught him a glancing blow along the side of his head. Svetlana followed it up, raining blows down upon the Brit. Two connected before Gray lashed out and shoved her away.

"I'm starting not to like you very much," he growled.

Svetlana glanced around for another weapon. Spying some hooks on the wall, she moved to rip one free and recommenced her attack. The point sliced through the air close to Gray's throat. He evaded the swipe.

"That's not nice," Gray said.

"Now who talks too much," Svetlana growled. And attacked again.

This time, Gray went low and hit her in the stomach. Svetlana stopped abruptly, and the former para reached out, grabbed her throat once more and drove her backward hard.

Svetlana made solid contact with the wall a loud smack. She went stiff, her eyes wide. Gray stared at her with curiosity. When he released her, she remained there, the wall hook securely embedded into her skull.

"You fucking pillock, you killed her."

Gray turned to Hawk. "It was an accident."

"Tell that to Anja."

"Fuck it."

"Alpha, copy?"

"Copy, Bravo. We lost you for a while there."

"Been busy. Send the helicopter, we're coming home."

"The package, Bravo One?"

"Negative, Alpha Two. No joy. The package is..."

He was about to say down hard but looked at Svetlana's upright figure. Instead, "...just hanging around."

"Say again, Bravo?"

But Hawk left it at that.

———

AFTER A FEW DAYS AT HOME, the mood of the team was still somber. Losing the White Dove had left the mission feeling like a loss. She could have played a pivotal role in repatriating the kidnap victims with their homes. Those who had been sold were still out there somewhere, and it was going to be an ongoing challenge to track them all down.

Hawk floated around on the air mattress while the others used their sun loungers. Gray took a pull of his beer and placed it on the table beside him. Movement from the villa drew his attention, and he smiled and rose from his lounger.

The blonde-haired woman took off her sunglasses and smiled back. "Got a beer for me?" asked Marlene Roth.

"Good to see you," Gray said.

The others turned their attention to the newcomer. Marlene greeted them. "Hello."

Ilse got to her feet. "Marlene, we weren't expecting you."

"I decided to surprise my sister. Is she around?"

"I'm right here," Anja said as she emerged from within the villa, holding a folder. She glared at the others. "I see you managed to evade our security."

All eyes went to Hawk. He reached for the gun tucked into his swim trunks. "I got my security right here."

Anja walked over to her sister and kissed her on the cheek. "Go in inside, Marlene, I'll be right with you."

Everyone was instantly on edge. As soon as Marlene was gone, Hawk asked, "What's happened?"

"The holding facility where Sergei Orlov was being held was attacked. Whoever did it was messy and left a bloody trail behind them. Ten dead and counting."

"Sounds familiar," Hawk replied.

"Yes. Kurt Runciman."

"What are we going to do, boss?"

She tossed the folder on the table in front of them as they gathered around. "Meet your next target."

"The Pale Crow," Ilse said.

"I'll never get used to that name," Slania said.

"He just inherited everything his father and sister had built up, becoming the biggest threat against women around the world we've ever encountered. Take a week, and we're going back to work."

ABOUT THE AUTHOR

A relative newcomer to the world of writing, Brent Towns self-published his first book, a western, in 2015. *Last Stand in Sanctuary* took him two years to write. His first hardcover book, a Black Horse Western, was published the following year.

Since then, he has written 26 western stories, including some in collaboration with British western author, Ben Bridges.

Also, he has written the novelization to the upcoming 2019 movie from One-Eyed Horse Productions, titled, *Bill Tilghman and the Outlaws*. Not bad for an Australian author, he thinks.

Brent Towns has also scripted three Commando Comics with another two to come.

He says, "The obvious next step for me was to venture into the world of men's action/adventure/thriller stories. Thus, Team Reaper was born."

A country town in Queensland, Australia, is where Brent lives with his wife and son.

In the past, he worked as a seaweed factory worker, a knife-hand in an abattoir, mowed lawns and tidied gardens, worked in caravan parks, and worked in the hire industry. And now, as well as writing books, Brent is a home tutor for his son doing distance education.

Brent's love of reading used to take over his life, now it's writing that does that; often sitting up until the small hours, bashing away at his tortured keyboard where he loses himself in the world of fiction.